I0565139

FOLLOW JEN

FOLLOW JEN

Scarlet
The Pimpernel retold

A Lady's Maid
Can she love again?

His Lady in Hiding
Hiding out as his maid.

Spun of Gold
Rumpelstilskin Retold

Dating the Duke
Time Travel: Regency man in NYC

Charmed by His Lordship
The antics of a fake friendship

Tabitha's Folly
Four over-protective brothers

To read Damen's Secret
The Villain's Romance

Follow her Newsletter

THE HEIR
AND SPARE

TWINS OF PEMBERLEY

JEN GEIGLE

JOHNSON

CHAPTER I
ELIZABETH

The carriage rocked back and forth as the wheels hit deep grooves in the road from the mud of last spring. But no one inside shifted at all with the movement. All five Bennet sisters and their mother and father were pressed together so tightly even the sisters who were nodding off to sleep were still sitting upright. Elizabeth was drowsy with a great need for sleep, but she knew her eyes would not close for many hours yet. Her face burned with a memory that would not soon leave. A slight from a man was something that stung, but a slight from a stranger, a wealthy stranger of noble birth, that was something else

1

entirely, and Elizabeth wasn't entirely certain how it sat with her.

"Not handsome enough to tempt me." The words echoed in Elizabeth's brain. She didn't know if she would ever erase from memory his insolent face or the sneer across his lips as he said them. By far the most fine-looking man in the room, gentlemen were scarce, and he couldn't even be bothered to dance with her? Jane was immediately captured by his friend. Elizabeth knew her sister, Jane, was superior in looks and grace and kindness and Lizzie may as well admit that she was by far the better choice for most men. But, certainly, there was a man somewhere who would prefer her, who would wish to be with her even when Jane was in the room. Or in this instance, could at least be tempted to dance a set.

She ground her teeth. She didn't begrudge Jane. Not at all. She wished her the very best happiness. Because Jane deserved it.

But she could be hurt and angry about such a slight without being jealous of her sister.

The carriage jerked to a stop. The overly tired Bennet sisters climbed out and stumbled onto their front porch and into the house. Even their mother was lulled into a subdued silence as the weight of the early hours of a morning after a night of dancing descended upon them all.

Jane's sleepy smile comforted Elizabeth. At least she'd been given the attention she desired. The apparently wealthy landowner, Bingley, had hardly taken his eyes off her, even when dancing with others. He'd showered Jane with smiles and attention and had walked her to their carriage as nearly the last people to leave the assembly.

No, Elizabeth didn't begrudge her sister her smiles. She smiled to herself. If her mother was correct, they would be hearing proposals in a week's time.

She rarely believed her mother on the subject of the Bennet women matrimony. She was far too desperate, far too concerned to have any sort of rational reaction to a potential suitor. She wanted it too badly. And in her own words, "You tell me what would occupy your thoughts if you had five daughters to marry who had no hopes of a living without?"

Elizabeth couldn't fault the woman. But she also didn't have to place too much trust in her opinions or predictions, either.

Left alone in the front entry, all others

making their way to their beds, the servants in tow, her thoughts reluctantly returned to Mr. Darcy. And to her horror, a lump filled her throat. She furiously dug fingernails into her palms. She would not give him the power to affect her so. She did not care. She couldn't. His opinion did not matter. And frankly, she was handsome. She was quite beautiful, she hoped. She'd thought she looked bright and cheery after a walk. Her eyes aglow with happiness, her cheeks rosy. She shook her head and fell to the couch, resting her head in her hands. She had thought she was comely enough when she left the house that morning. Handsome enough to dance with.

She rose to her feet and began pacing. What she hated most was that she was having this internal conversation at all. No man should have that kind of power over her thoughts, over her feelings for herself. She moved to a mirror and studied her face, turning this way and that to see all the angles. She supposed if viewed from the left, her nose looked a bit...off. She adjusted the angle. But really, from most other viewpoints she was quite lovely even after a long night of dancing. She pursed her lips. Was she lying to herself? Was she really quite plain? Her shoulders slumped and the light of expectancy dimmed. Perhaps when she didn't think anyone was looking, she morphed into an unadmirable visage that no one wanted. She glanced in the mirror to try and catch such an image to see if it were true. But no. She really did not look plain. She had striking features and they were lovely. She stood taller. And what she usually cared for more, was her wit. And her intelligence. She loved sparring. She loved a good play with words and understanding. She loved a good book. She hungered for information. And she loved how quickly she picked up on her father's humor.

And what's more? She was proud of her long walks and her ability to see things logically. She was proud of her pen. She could write witty quips and long letters that had her sisters buckled over in tears. She was excellent at expressing herself when she wished to. She nodded; her eyes carried a familiar glint of confidence she welcomed back. And then her anger returned. The fact that a man, a stranger she hardly knew, created such a crisis of self confidence in her with one phrase, one sentiment, angered her. She could not be giving others that kind of power. No. She would not.

She continued on this line of thought, walking back and forth across the room, ignoring the mirror. By the time she'd paced for a few minutes, she'd worked through the insecurity and had worked herself up into some serious self-love and obstinate determination to block out his words forever. She was handsome enough but more than that, she was enough period, smart enough, happy enough, resourceful enough, enough. The real question was not to determine her worth, but his. Was *he* enough?

With that new direction, she nodded to herself again in the mirror and at last went to bed.

Jane was already asleep, her smile lingering even in slumber.

Tomorrow she would exert her energy toward Jane.

And she needed to find her best friend, Charlotte. They were long overdue a conversation.

As she drifted off to sleep, one unresolved thought remained. Even after it all, she did find him handsome. Too bad his personality ruined such a perfect face.

CHAPTER 2
ARTHUR DARCY

While Fitzwilliam spent a diverting holiday with Bingley in his new estate, Arthur Darcy, his twin brother, spent the morning working on his ledgers. Really, it was Fitzwilliam's responsibility, but did Fitz ever do anything he was supposed to be doing? Not unless it was under the pretense of finding a wife. Arthur scoffed. Finding a wife apparently covered every instance of socializing that his brother ever did, including his recent travels to Netherfield under the guise of helping his friend set up house. Arthur knew he was neither finding a wife nor assisting at Netherfield, but merely avoiding Pemberley. He could only hope he was not insulting all and sundry as he had lately taken to doing. His brother really was a lovely person. He was just supremely bothered of late.

Arthur frowned. What on earth would Fitz find of use in that area? What wife was he hoping to find there? Arthur was the brother who would find interest in the smaller towns. He would love a simple woman who loved to read, who took care of herself but did not spend too much time or energy on the latest in fashions. She didn't know about pomades or hair rods or anything too complicated but simply awoke with freshness and light in her face; had eyes shining with the peace of good living and smiled easily with the joy of their relationship. He shook his head. Such a woman was not to be found in London. At least not that Arthur had yet encountered.

London did have many women of fashion, experts in the wiles of capturing men. And Fitz fit right in with that crowd. So what he was doing in the wilds of Netherfield was a surprise to Arthur.

Everyone knew that Fitz had no intention of settling down any time soon. Which was perhaps why he'd hidden himself away in such a remote location.

Really the man could do what he pleased, when he wished. Arthur had no need for him to do anything with the estate at the moment. He preferred when his brother stayed far away from estate decisions even though one day it would be his to manage. As the older twin he would receive it all, be the new keeper of everything, all the tenants, the servants and the legacy that was the Darcy name. Fitz was the heir.

The longer Arthur set things in motion to protect the income from mismanagement, the better. But he did wish the man to at least produce an heir.

He grimaced and then let his head fall into his hands. He was sounding like his grandmother, his mother, his aunt Lady Catherine. He was sounding like every other matron in the London *Ton* with eyes on the men to start marrying. With head still in hands, he counted to one hundred. It really was time for him to get out more. There were other things to be concerned with besides the estate. His own finding of a wife, for example.

He would not inherit the estate. He would

not be the one doing the books always, but he had ensured his own inheritance. He'd ensured a living for himself, one that would be very profitable—not Pemberley, but it could one day become something really special.

His father had left him that much, for which he was grateful. He and whomever he chose to marry would be doing well indeed.

But it pained him to lose Pemberley. And he felt that he certainly would within a generation after Fitz took over the helm.

He raised his head and closed the ledger, slowly, carefully, and then placed it back in the drawer near his right thigh. He might lose PemberleyPemberley, but his own estate would be in good stead. That much he could control.

And he'd leave Pemberley in the best possible place for when his brother took the helm.

His servant Thomas entered the room with a tray. "You have some correspondence." He approached. "And Mrs. Godley would like to know if you are ready for your repast?"

It was time he left his office. He needed air and sunshine and a good hard ride on Samson his old faithful stallion. He'd purchased a few more horses to add to his stable, knowing Samson could not live forever. But he would never tire of his old friend of a horse as long as he could still ride. "I think I'd like to take my tea on the back veranda."

"Very good sir." He bowed and waited while Arthur took the letters from his tray.

He sorted them by business and social engagements. Usually his pile was filled with business and his brother's social, but there were a few notable invitations directed solely to him.

He raised his eyebrows. One particular was odd in every way. He was invited to a house party, in the general vicinity of Netherfield. From Lord Shackley? A man no one ever saw. A man who was most respected as an old relic of an earlier era. He'd been a close friend of the Darcys' father. But no one had seen him in years. An eccentric older noble had planned a house party? And for whatever reason, he'd chosen to invite Arthur to his gathering? He almost tossed it aside to be turned down by his steward, but something made him hesitate. He reached for it again, studying the letters as if they would help him solve the puzzle. Perhaps Fitz would like to attend. Surely Lord Shackley wouldn't care which twin supported his efforts. Some loyalty to his father prevented Arthur from dismissing the invitation outright. Yes, this was something he'd ask Fitz to attend, to prove his efforts at wife finding. Who knew but there would be someone there to catch his brother's eye.

He locked his office before heading out to the veranda. Cook had made his favorite pies. He smiled. Bless the woman. They all worked a little better, a little harder when he was home. And he appreciated them. They were like family. He could hardly look at Cook without thinking of his mother poring over recipes with her as they planned meals for dinners and parties. The cozy sensations that filled him at that thought had him pondering again on the house party. Perhaps there would be a woman there for him? There had to be a reason he'd been invited instead of his brother. Surely there was something unique for him? The area was more country. Close enough to London to draw some of that crowd naturally, but perhaps some from the local countryside as well. Someone unknown by others, a gem in the wilds of the British country? He'd love someone not taught in the wiles of man-seeking, honestly, or someone also not particularly proficient in gossip either. Was this house party a place to find such a woman? There was no reason why he would be on Lord Shackley's mind. He'd not been near him or anything he involved himself in for many years.

And yet, here he was being invited.

Did he believe in fate? Not usually. But in this case, he wondered. And the enticing question of *what if* had snagged his curiosity and was not letting go. He lifted a cup to his mouth and savored tea made to his precise preference. But not made by his wife, made by his servant. It was time to find someone to fill his lonely days, to share his nights, to work side by side in the care of their estate, someone with whom he could build a legacy.

He dabbed his lips. The time had come for him to find such a woman. And he already knew she was not to be found in London. Perhaps this house party was just the thing.

Instead of asking his steward to handle it, he responded himself. He had two months to prepare. But come August, he would be attending Lord Shackley's party.

CHAPTER 3

ELIZABETH

E lizabeth and Jane walked through the back edges of their property where Elizabeth knew wild herbs and roots grew. Their baskets were only partly filled, but they hadn't as yet come across the lavender.

Jane lifted a delicate lace flower from a bush and placed it in her basket. "We are so fortunate that the conditions are so favorable for many of these."

"We really are. And of course that the past vicar taught us how to plant them."

Elizabeth dug out the roots of a particularly useful herb. "We will need to plant more of this one if it's the roots we need every time."

"I think the leaves and flowers are also useful. But I think you're correct. We must plant some more. They aren't spreading like they could." She pressed her lips together. "I think it might be the lack of sun. See those branches? They weren't there when we originally began this plot of our wild garden."

Lizzie nodded. "I see what you mean."

"Let's have Joshua come and trim those." Jane seemed to be doing her mental calculations about all the branches she would ask him to trim. Lizzie let her handle it. She was pleased they could work on this together and that she was so intrigued by the idea of them growing their own medicines. The vicar had been correct and his remedies worked. Particularly the one to quell their mother's nerves. She was much more relaxed. And complained so infrequently of the flutterings and flittings of her heart that Lizzie almost forgot her constant need for smelling salts.

They moved toward the field. "But look! That lavender is beautiful." They paused at the edge of the trees. Their lavender had definitely spread and now filled a rather large patch with a thick flowing wave of color. The sweet aroma tickled her nose and she breathed deeply. "And this must be Mother Nature's trophy. It's almost a shame to pick some."

"This will certainly grow." Jane ran her fingers over the tops of the flowers. "It will make a beautiful water."

"And it's supposed to be good for calming us as well as Mother you know, perhaps a sachet under our pillows?"

"Or Lydia's pillow." Jane laughed. "That girl could use some calming."

"I think perhaps when the militia is not in town, she will go back to bemoaning her boredom."

"We can only hope." Jane clipped a stalk of lavender.

Once their baskets were full of all sorts of aromatic herbs and plants, they turned to walk back up the hill to the house.

"Tell me." Lizzie searched the side of Jane's face as they walked. "How was the lunch with Bingley's sisters?"

Jane's face grew troubled, and Lizzie almost regretted asking.

"They are...not as congenial as he." She walked along in silence for a moment, but Lizzie didn't pressure her.

She stopped suddenly. "In fact, I do believe they are openly insulting if you want to know the truth."

Lizzie gasped. "What did they do to you? Did they insult you? Surely not with Bingley right there?"

"Oh no, nothing at all, not really." She sighed. "You know those people who say nothing at all, not really, but they are saying so much. They leave so much to be assumed and to hurt." Her face clouded further and lizzie was shocked to see a tear form at the corner of her eyes.

"What is this?" She pulled Jane into a hug. "What did they say or not say or whatever?"

"Oh, just things like, 'Your mother would know about laughing.'"

Lizzie paused and frowned. "Wait, that's it?"

"You know, because she was laughing so hard she had that coughing fit at the assembly and then she was so loud about me and Bingley, about us courting even before we knew one another." She fisted a portion of her dress in her hand. "I'm sorry. I should be more loyal to our mother, but that was so embarrassing. Bingley heard, and we could hardly look at one another. He looked everywhere but at me. Then Caroline said things about Lydia too; about Mary's playing the piano and her less than impressive voice. She said all kinds of things without saying anything at all and when I left I felt that every part of me was lacking in some way."

"She talked about you as well? About me?"

"Well no. We were left off her list of people to criticize. But even Father. She hardly saw him at all but she had things to not say about him as well."

Lizzie stomped her feet as she walked. "I really hate that kind of talk. Everyone seems so proficient at insulting in the most polite manner possible. I don't often know how to counter it. If one is overly careful in their wording, never quite saying what you think they might be saying, how do you even respond without turning the conversation into something childish or brutish?" She frowned.

"Well, no matter. We don't want to claim a proficiency in insulting others, do we?"

Lizzie laughed and then wrapped her free

arm over Jane's shoulder. "No, we do not. And you, my dear, could never be such a thing no matter if you desired it. But I." She shook her head. "I feel...I am well on my way." She tucked a strand of free hair behind her ear. "You must somehow disbelieve everything they insinuated and remember them to be the most boring, insipid creatures we have yet encountered. Who would want to be in the presence of a perpetual bored expression and a tight pinched face? She couldn't be lovely with those evil thoughts running through her head. No one could. She will be doomed to ill looks and you will forever be fresh and lovely and a pleasure to look upon until your dying day." She kissed her soundly on the cheek.

Jane laughed, pretending to wipe the offending gesture from her cheek. "I think you are also perfectly perfect and do not need to think ill of yourself. Though you have more wit than I, you would never purposefully be cruel, not like they were. I know this." She toyed with a ringlet of Lizzie's hair. "And thank you for that. Thank you for always being my strength and having my back."

"We are quite a pair, are we not? We shall

rise together or go down trying." She laughed. "But truly. I do think Bingley is half in love with you no matter what his sisters say."

"He does have a glorious sparkle in his eye." Jane laughed, her face blushing profusely. "Is that how you tell? If a man loves you...does he sparkle like Bingley?"

"I'm not the one to ask as no one has loved me as of yet. But what I see in Bingley is definitely a high interest. He seems completely captured, living in the world of Jane Bennet, not aware of any other world. I would say that is half in love." Lizzie grinned. "And yes, he does seem to have an extra sparkle for you."

Jane nodded, seeming satisfied with that answer. And Lizzie hoped that none of his friend's snobbery would rub off on him for she feared that her sister was herself if not half, all the way in love already.

They returned to the house with baskets of herbs and things for Cook which were soon almost forgotten in the wake of callings and shoutings from their mother.

Lizzie groaned. "What could be happening now?"

Jane shrugged, and they both left the baskets

on the table in the kitchen and went following the noise.

Their mother was on her back in her bed, fanning her overly pale face. "Oh, my dear Jane, we are so unfairly treated! So unfairly. And here I thought that my Lydia would amount to something, would be able to have the same amount of opportunity as her sisters. But how can she? How? When she is so roundly ignored?" She clutched a paper, an invitation of sorts.

"What is that, Mama?" Jane reached for it.

At first her mother resisted. "No, I will not allow it. How could this Lord I-don't-even-know-his-name include Mary but not our Lydia? What is he thinking?"

Jane and Lizzie shared a confused glance.

Lizzie reached for the paper and this time her mother let it go. The sisters skimmed the page.

"Elizabeth and Mary Bennet have been invited to the house party of one Lord Shackley. The pleasure of your presence is expected on August 1."

Elizabeth let the paper drop, her eyes unseeing. What could this mean? She and Mary were invited to a house party? "Who is Lord Shackley?"

Before her mother could begin wailing anew, her father's voice interrupted behind them. "He is a colleague of mine. We correspond weekly on all manner of topics. He's an eccentric to be sure but a brilliant mind. You will find his wit delicious, and his knowledge of the world is unmatched. I'm quite envious, actually." He smiled and reached for his daughter's hand. "As for why he chose the two of you, I cannot say. But I suggest you enjoy yourselves. It promises to be highly diverting if not quizzical at times. And I would guess his invitation to include some fine minds indeed."

Lizzie nodded, her interest and curiosity definitely piqued.

Mary stepped forward, glancing nervously at their mama. "Am I to go then? Truly?" She showed the tiniest spark of hope as if she daren't but wished to.

Her mother commenced wailing again. "Oh, my Lydia! Never to have an opportunity like the rest of you and by far the prettiest outside of Jane." She clutched her eldest daughter's hands. "It is not for nothing you are so lovely. Bingley will marry you and save us all, mark my words." Her eyes were wide and desperate.

Lizzie looked to her father. What were they to do?

He shook his head and stepped out into the hall. Mary and Lizzie followed. "I do believe your invitations are due to my intimacy with him. We are quite close by letter. And he knows of all my daughters. Perhaps he knew you to be the most appreciative of his humor or his library." Her father winked. "Either way, it will be a good diversion will it not?"

Mary nodded and clutched her hands to her chest. "I shall treasure every moment. Do you think he will appreciate a good sermon?"

Her father chuckled. "I cannot say. We have not been overly communicative about the things of the cloth. But I daresay someone there might wish to humor you." He patted her hand, sharing a glance with Lizzie. "Follow your sister's good example in her decorum and conversation. She will lead you well."

Lizzie tried to wrap her mind around this new turn. She was intrigued. And curious. And it provided such a different diversion to her normal predictable life she admitted to being quite excited. "So, he has an impressive library you assume?"

Her father's eyes twinkled. "Judging by his correspondence, I would guess one of the best. He is quite knowledgeable on many different topics and quotes different authors as though they are dear friends."

Lizzie could tell by the way he lingered in thought that he treasured this correspondence. She wondered just how much influence he had exerted to gain an invitation. But she was grateful. It would be good to get away. Especially with her dear Jane so well situated and being courted by Bingley. She could avoid the awful Darcy and still hope the best for his friend.

She kissed Jane on the cheek as she hummed with a little skip down the hall to call for a trunk to be brought to her room.

The next day was filled with preparations for the two girls to leave. It was not often they were invited to do anything outside of Longbourne. In fact, none had ever been to a house party. Their mother had stopped wailing and eventually left her room to exert herself in the girls' behalf. She had many thoughts on colors to wear and which bonnets to bring. She even had the girls bring their newer ball gowns just in case. By the time they were loading into the carriage, she had even summoned a smile and a hope for Mary to do really well. "If you smile more, my dear, you shall find the man for you. I'm sure there is one who loves to read and carry on about Fordyce's sermons the way you do." She dabbed her eyes. Though she didn't sound very convincing, Mary seemed cheered by her words.

Lizzie put an arm across her shoulders. "Don't worry, sister. We shall find much with which to divert ourselves, I'm certain of it."

"I daren't breathe wrong for fear she will stop my going."

"Never fear. Father is right there ensuring our departure." She smiled warmly at him. "Thank you. We shall write when we arrive."

"And do make a note of all that is ridiculous so that we may divert ourselves later."

"I will. But perhaps it shall not be as ridiculous as it is fanciful. Or even fun." She winked, and then she and Mary stepped up into the carriage.

Her sister breathed out in relief as soon as they started moving and then her tears began to fall. "Shall I really be allowed to attend? I cannot believe it." She wiped at her eyes, but the tears kept flowing.

"Oh, my dear." Lizzie moved to sit at her side. "Of course we are off. We are moving, see? Father has made sure of it."

She sniffed again and again but eventually the tears stopped, and she leaned into Lizzie with a smile. "I think this shall be the happiest times of my life. I shall not want to leave."

Lizzie squeezed her. "We shall experience them together whatever they may be. I'm quite as excited as you, I think. At least for the library."

"And who knows but the others who are invited have a predilection for books too? Or something in common with us?" Mary lifted out a novel.

"What is this? Are you reading fiction now?"

"I thought I should so that I know how to function in these sorts of activities, how men wish to be handled, how to fall in love." Her face turned as bright red as Lizzie had ever seen it. "I'm ridiculous I know. But I'm desperately uneducated in the ways of romance."

"As am I, my dear. I think fiction is a good choice for you but not because you need to change your ways. You just smile like Father said and be yourself. You'll find someone who enjoys you just the way you are." She was gratified to see the relief in Mary's expression.

She opened the book to the second chapter. "All the same. I shall try to be the most approachable and knowable, pleasant version of myself. How's that?"

"I think that is very savvy of you. Quite a great way of putting it. I shall do the same, how about that?"

Mary nodded, pleased. "If I learn anything of import in my book, I shall let you know."

"What are you reading?"

She held up the title page. "It's called *Pride and Prejudice*." She ginned. "And so far, the hero is the most unlikable creature. But he has potential." She tapped her finger on her lips. "I should not mind a curmudgeonly type of person if I understood him." She lifted the book again then paused. "As long as he was kind, in his heart; kind but a little bit grumpy? That would be all right."

Lizzie laughed. "What an odd and very Mary thing to say." She didn't know how much she'd want to marry a disagreeable man. The insult from earlier did not sting as much as it had, but she was still struck by how much a rejection like that with harsh words could affect her. No, she was not hoping to find a disagreeable man. Hopefully she would be enough for whoever was at the house party. They did not have to marry after all, or even dance perhaps. But they would be paired off doing activities together, presumably. She'd asked about house parties and all her mother could remember was that they were planned out carefully with fun diversions for the guests, and seating for meals and the numbers were typically even, so there would be men there, single men. And perhaps new friends in the women. She needed the diversion. She was not perhaps as desperate as Mary, but she was more than grateful to be rid of Mr. Darcy and his critical eye and rejections. It had affected her more than she realized.

At any rate, ready or not, they would be arriving in an hour or two. They were not too far from home which also brought some semblance of comfort. If it turned out to be full of disagreeable and grumpy people, she and Mary could leave no matter how much her sister was appreciating the grumpy but kind men. She laughed to herself. "Dear Mary. We shall have an adventure of it, that much I can promise."

Mary hugged her book closer and Elizabeth looked out over the top of her head to watch the green hills out the window as their carriage made it slowly down the road toward Lord Shackley's estate. Yes, an adventure indeed.

CHAPTER 4

ARTHUR DARCY

rthur arrived at Lord Shackley's early in the afternoon. The activities weren't supposed to begin until evening, but he liked to situate himself, and he had some correspondence to take care of before the other guests arrived. Besides, he also hoped to re-acquaint himself with the elusive Lord Shackley. What had he been doing with himself these past quieter years? How had he thought anew of Arthur, and why was he invited? He smiled to himself. All things he hoped to know from the host who had not yet shown himself.

He'd been taken excellent care of even so. The servants had led him to a lovely well-appointed room with a view of the expansive property and the front drive. He'd refreshed himself, his valet had unpacked his things and settled in the extra room attached to his closet. It was all very convenient and comfortable. He was pleased indeed.

A maid scratched at the door and his valet opened it, bringing in a tray. "For your enjoyment. Dinner will be later this evening."

"Thank you." Darcy smiled. This was very comfortable indeed. "My gratitude to our host."

Sounds of a carriage arriving caught his attention. "Ah." He stood at the window. He also had a clear and easy view of every arriving guest. His curiosity was definitely piqued. Who did Lord Shackley know? Who would Darcy be sharing the house party with?

The carriage seemed old, but well taken care of, the horses a fine team. He stepped closer to the window as the equipage stopped just below. Would he see the people stepping down?

Two bonnets descended the carriage steps, one at a time. They were colorful, prettily dressed as all women were, but Darcy could ascertain nothing else about them. He was about to step back from the window to continue his final letter when one of them looked up and met his eyes. He froze. Caught staring? But her expression captured him. She was curious, intelligent, light, and something more, something fleeting as though she might be off and running through a field if left to her own devices. She held his gaze but a moment more, and then her mouth dropped and she frowned. Whipping her skirts about her, she tugged on her companion and then entered the house with firm and hurried steps.

What on earth had that been about? Did he know her? How could he? And he knew of no women who would frown so openly at him. He'd not offended any that he knew. Perhaps, despite his initial interest in her upturned mouth and pert nose, she was not as pleasant as he hoped.

He stepped back from the window as their trunks were unloaded. He'd be wary of her until he knew more, certainly.

His tray of food was delicious; fine cheeses, chocolate even, strong tea and a selection of fine tarts that dissolved on his tongue. It was rare to find a chef as good as the one they'd convinced to join them at Pemberley from France. But here Lord Shackley had fine food. And Arthur hadn't known how much he cared for fine food until he found it outside his home. He dabbed his mouth. Yes, it was a treat indeed.

There was a knock at his door. When he opened it, a footman bowed. "The pleasure of your attention is requested in Lord Shackley's east library, if it pleases you."

"Excellent." Arthur was good and ready to see any library this man might have. "Lead the way."

"Very good, Mr. Darcy."

A soft gasp captured his attention from down the hall but when he looked, he saw only closed doors. He brushed off his shoulder one time, more out of habit than anything. His valet would never let him be dressed in anything other than the finest cared-for articles of clothing, even though Arthur insisted that he use them to their point of breaking before acquiring new garments. He did not wish to waste. His brother did enough of that.

He walked down well-worn wood floors that shined with care, slightly uneven beneath his feet. The walls were lit by candles in sconces; now and then a bundle of flowers filled the hall with a fresh aroma. Did they have a greenhouse? Where were they cultivating the flowers? He'd have to explore the gardens. He was most interested in all things out of doors, naturally. And in the library of course. And in their host.

He had high hopes to meet a lovely country girl as well, but the frowning one doused his excitement somewhat. He did not wish to be fooled by a smiling miss who frowned at strangers.

Memories from his childhood he tried not to relive clouded his brain. There was no need to think of his mother's bouts with the blues and the angries. He didn't know what else to call them. His nurse had been a godsend and had made a game of it. "Be careful, the angries are out. Best to stay put for the morning." But when his mother let her emotions overtake her judgment, she was a different person indeed. And he had tried to steer clear of her path but had been caught in her fire enough times to know he did not wish to experience the cruel and illogical wrath of any other woman.

Luckily his sister was everything that was good and sweet natured. She was giving and hopeful and full of innocent caring. He'd love for someone with even a bit more challenge in her voice, with wit and daring—but kindness. Always kindness.

He shook his head. Perhaps this was not the week to find such a woman but it was definitely time for him to start looking, to make a real effort in that direction at least. It would do his sister Georgiana well and perhaps rid his thoughts of the echoes of what should be there. Always missing someone, always a hole where someone should be. Arthur was lonely. It came down to something as simple as that. He was lonely.

They approached a bright and airy opened doorway where sunlight spilled out into the hall. He liked the room already.

The servant entered ahead of him to announce, "A Mr. Arthur Darcy, my lord." With a bow, he turned to leave them be.

Arthur stepped into the room and bowed to a wizened older man with a bright smile. "Lord Shackley." When he rose, the man stepped forward with his hand outstretched. "Darcy, good to see you."

"You as well, my lord. I only wish I could be giving you the well wishes from my father. But surely he would be happy to see a valued acquaintance renewed. He enjoyed your conversations, I know that."

"Yes, he was a dear friend, a challenging intellect and an excellent conversationalist."

Arthur nodded. "I was so pleased to come. How have you been? Your estate is well situated, comfortable. I've had every need accommodated."

"Excellent." He nodded, seeming pleased, but also not needing the praise. "We are just waiting on two others and we will begin." He smiled. "We expect all our guests to arrive by late this evening, but the three of you who are here are fortuitous."

Arthur thought that an interesting choice of words, particularly if he referred to the frowning woman who had arrived recently.

And then they entered. The footman announced, "Misses Elizabeth and Mary Bennet."

Their curtseys were lovely and well-practiced. They carried themselves with perfect poise. But Miss Elizabeth could not hide a certain stoicism in her expression before she turned her face down to perform her curtsey.

He stepped forward to reach for her hand.

She offered it with a completely blank expression. No smile, no surprise, nothing. "Mr. Darcy."

He bowed over her hand, lightly kissing her knuckles. "Miss Elizabeth?"

She nodded and then turned to her side. "I don't know if you've met my sister Mary?"

It seemed an odd choice of words and action. He'd not met Miss Elizabeth either, had he? Why was she introducing her sister to him? But he shrugged it off and bowed over Miss Mary's hand next, brushing his lips across her gloved knuckles. "It is a pleasure, Misses Mary and Elizabeth. I look forward to our time together with such an illustrious host." He smiled.

Miss Elizabeth seemed curious, and with an odd questioning expression she turned to their host. "And you must be Lord Shackley?"

The older gentleman grinned. "Yes!" He clapped his hands together, his eyes crinkling with evidence of frequent smiles. "The daughters of one of my most cherished correspondents. Welcome. I'm so pleased he could spare you."

He seemed to surprise them with a grandfatherly type hug. "I feel as if you are my own. He speaks so highly and so often of you both. But you don't know me yet. Thank you for humoring an old man and coming to brighten my days."

Miss Elizabeth's face changed into a beacon of happiness, and Darcy's mouth went dry. In that moment, she was the most beautiful woman he had ever seen, surely. Her eyes lit, her smile was large and full, her nose pert, wrinkled just around the end as though finding something so delightful she couldn't withhold the happiness. He was enchanted.

But when she turned back to him and saw his face, everything in her expression dimmed. He couldn't account for it, but the difference was so stark, some explanation must be owed.

Lord Shackley cleared his throat and looked between them for a moment then said, "Come, let me give you a tour of my collections as we await one other who has not yet arrived." He looked at Miss Mary as if to say she might find the new arrival most interesting and then continued his sentence. "You four will certainly find the most enjoyment from my tomes." He held out his arm toward one section of the wall. "Let's begin with the masters."

The room was lined with books as one

would expect, and smelled of books which Darcy quite enjoyed. It reminded him of his study at home. But it also held very interesting busts and other items on the shelves. The books were not organized by any sort of size or color, but by subject matter or author it seemed. It made for a more eclectic looking experience. If Miss Elizabeth's pleased expression were anything to go by, she quite enjoyed it. He tried to, but his fingers itched to start moving things around. The one book taller than the rest for example. What was it doing there? Standing tall, asking to be moved, begging to find a home on the other side of the shelf with the others of its height. He stepped nearer but before he could begin a bit of reorganizing, Lord Shackley directed their attention to a particular book with a dark green binding he held in his hands.

"This, my friends, will become very familiar to all of you."

They all stepped closer.

Miss Elizabeth brushed against his arm and then flinched away, stepping so obviously far from him he had to wonder again if he'd done something to offend her in some way. He dipped his head in an effort to apologize for accidentally being in her space.

But she wasn't looking. She was so actively avoiding looking at him that her face was turned away from even their host as he attempted to show them a new set of books.

If it were possible to look somewhere besides at him, she was actively doing it. He stared at her, wondering if she would give up and glance his way.

"What are you doing?" Her whisper sounded soft, but her expression was anything but.

"I'm wondering if you might glance my way again. I want to be ready for it."

Her lips twitched.

And he smiled. So she had a sense of humor.

At last she turned to him, her eyes smiling. "There. I'm looking. Now, we should be paying more attention to that book with the green binding."

Miss Mary had it in her clutches and she did look as though she might never let it go.

"Why exactly are we to be so interested in this particular piece of literature?" He wished to sequester the two of them off for a moment now that she was smiling in his direction.

"I believe, if you were listening, you would have heard that we are to create a theatrical endeavor of some sort...a musical or a play or simply a reading." She crossed her arms. "And we are paired to do it."

He coughed and then attempted to hide his enjoyment so as not to alienate her again. "Oh? And tell me, how are your performing abilities?"

"Paltry at best. I'm afraid I might be the weak link of the two of us?"

"Not at all I'm certain, as I have very little ability in any of the areas needed. Perhaps we shall work on a comedy of errors?"

She tapped her finger on the tip of her nose. "I think you're on to something."

Their host seemed oblivious to them both except for the occasional glance out the side of his eye. Whatever his goal was for this activity, he was certainly actively interested in their reaction. He hovered over Miss Mary, answering questions and turning through the pages. But he was definitely aware of Miss Elizabeth and himself. How very curious. Well, he should be grateful to the man. He'd very much like to get to know this new Miss Elizabeth and to keep her frowns at bay.

The door to the library opened with a rather large bang, jerking their attention toward a slightly disheveled young man standing in the doorway, waving aside the servant who had followed and was about to announce him.

"I'm Lord Perceval." He bowed with a flourish of one hand. "I apologize for my tardiness."

"Oh, excellent. I told them to expect your arrival." Lord Shackley's grin could hardly be contained as he looked from Miss Mary to the newcomer and back.

Miss Elizabeth snorted and then covered her face with one hand. "Excuse me."

"No, my sentiments exactly." He nodded in Lord Perceval's direction. Then he held out his hand. "I'm Mr. Darcy. This is Miss Elizabeth and Miss Mary."

They shook hands and then with the same flourish and dramatics, Lord Perceval bowed over Miss Elizabeth's hand. He lingered a moment longer than one would expect, long enough to draw attention, and then rose with a wink just for her.

Arthur wished to stand between them. But

Miss Elizabeth seemed unfazed by this stranger's attempt to flirt with her.

He knew he had no right to prevent such a gesture, so he tamped down his protective reaction, somewhat.

Then Lord Perceval primped and played with Miss Mary for a moment. Darcy soon saw that the playful nature was simply his manner of interacting. And Darcy hoped the women could see such a thing as well, that Miss Mary's heart would be guarded, and that Miss Elizabeth would still enjoy Arthur's rather quiet and subdued manner after such an energetic force entered the room.

CHAPTER 5

ELIZABETH

Elizabeth watched Mary with astonishment as she blushed and giggled and warmed under the flamboyant energy that poured out of Lord Perceval. Mary might not be enamored, but she was indeed enjoying herself. And Mary enjoying herself was not something Elizabeth could remember happening. Ever. She had supposed that Mary's version of enjoyment was limited to the more serious pursuits of thought and action and that she was very much above anything frivolous. But Lord Perceval was able to find the part of Mary that did indeed enjoy attention and a social conversation.

Elizabeth felt like one of those tittering

marms who watched from the side and match-made every couple that came together. Nothing slipped by those women. But she could not help her riveted attention.

Lord Shackley approached them. "I do have another copy of the green volume."

"Oh, thank you."

Lord Perceval and Mary moved with the book to sit by the fire, and Elizabeth didn't think that conversation was ending any time soon.

* * *

Elizabeth and Mr. Darcy found their own corner of the room. He stood behind a chair for Elizabeth and when she was seated, sat as close as was possible to her. "I would like to at least see who is the author of such an intriguing tome? And how will we adapt the stories in some theatrical way?"

He rubbed his hands together in such an outward show of glee that Elizabeth could only laugh.

Mr. Darcy watched her, and as she glanced again in his direction was stunned by the appreciative smile and sparkle in his eyes.

Could this be the same man who couldn't be bothered to dance with her? Was this the one who deemed her not handsome enough? What had caused such a transformation? Was it simply because she was the only woman of interest present? Would his attention drift once the others arrived? She couldn't know, but decided there was no reason to continue with antagonism. She would simply keep her distance emotionally and certainly guard her heart against such a handsome face, one who was showing an extra amount of attention. Being noticed, she decided, was heady. A man's attention to her every intake of breath, his eyes studying the curls of her hair, the curve of her lips, was sending waves of anticipation through her in such a way that she wanted more and felt herself drawn to him simply because he saw her. Never before had she known you could sense a man's eyes on you, feel where he looked, respond to his gaze. She warmed and knew her face was turning pink. It was heady indeed.

Lord Shackley brought them another book, a copy of the same in Mary's hands. Elizabeth opened it up and smiled. "*Shakespeare's Sonnets?*"

"Exactly. Think of all you can do with that! Think of the possibilities."

Mr. Darcy rubbed his chin. "Could we also

glean from the actual stories? They might be easier to portray?"

"You may, certainly, as long as the sonnets play a part. They must be central."

Elizabeth turned page after page and then laughed to herself. "They are some of the most romantic..." She cleared her throat. "*That God forbid who made me first your slave?*" She ran her finger down the page. "*Sweet love renew thy force...thus can my love excuse the slow offense...shall I compare thee to a summer's day...*" She paused and glanced up at Lord Shackley. "Are you perchance hoping to enliven the romantic tendencies of this group?"

"Naturally." He winked. "But with poetry, it is surely a stout way to douse love rather than enliven it, don't you agree?"

She tipped her head. "I do indeed. Though it is a rare person who agrees with me."

Mr. Darcy frowned. "Isn't poetry the stuff of which love is fanned and flamed?"

"Of a stout love, perhaps. But any paltry beginning love will surely be stifled and find it too disagreeable a diversion as to alienate both parties."

His brow furrowed. "So, we should halt before we begin?"

"That depends, Mr. Darcy. How sturdy is our love?"

His mouth dropped and his face drained of color. "Pardon me?"

But Elizabeth laughed until she coughed. "Oh, Mr. Darcy. I am merely teasing. I have no inclination of a love between us. I am merely attempting to make this seem less awkward. Am I failing terribly?"

His face was a charming rosy color which she never imagined to ever see on Mr. Darcy, but he nodded as if attempting to gain control again of his emotions. "We shall persevere, Miss Elizabeth, and find that perhaps I am handsome enough to overcome whatever weakness the Bard might bring to our young and fragile friendship?"

She felt herself bristle and before she could stop herself from responding said, "Handsome enough? You may well be. But what is handsome enough to tempt you, Mr. Darcy?"

His brow lowered. "I'm afraid I don't understand. Perhaps my wit is not as worthy to follow?" His confusion was a puzzle to her. Had he no memory of her really? They'd not mentioned yet their previous knowledge of one another. Was she so inconsequential that he'd forgotten her altogether?

"Handsome enough to tempt me?" He searched her face for some elusive answer to the questions he obviously had. "I suppose there might be many things..." He stumbled over the words. "What about you?"

She shook her head. "I don't know. I find the whole concept to be entirely too prideful in nature. Who deems people worthy of dancing, or handsome enough for attention." She frowned and looked away. Suddenly all the previous ease they'd had, all the fun in smiles and flirtatious ground they'd gained fizzled away in the memory of his insult. And to think she'd not been handsome enough to even be remembered. She turned away. "Perhaps we should take turns reading it? You can go first and choose one for us to do?"

"Oh, well, certainly I can do whatever you wish. Might it be more enjoyable to read together..." His voice trailed off as she looked away, her frown deepening.

"Very well." He lifted the book and sat back

in his chair. He was silent for many moments and the uncomfortable feeling in the room grew. How could he have forgotten her? How could they openly use the same words and he not remember? What had not been handsome enough for him? She clasped her hands together in supreme annoyance. Then she stood and walked about the room. Mary was reading closely with her partner. They seemed perfectly in sync and happy with their pairing. They'd been able to function, to keep a friendly rapport. Why could she not do the same? Why must she overcomplicate everything?

When she turned back over her shoulder to see what he was doing, he was still engrossed in the book, with not a care for their situation or for her.

She told herself that he was only doing as she so clearly indicated. That who would want to read close with a woman who was angry at him, who openly frowned in his direction? But all the same, he could at least attempt to look in her direction again?

She knew he would not. A man could only put up with her supreme prejudice before his pride prevented him from pursuing further.

But had she not a right to be irritated, to not trust him, to already know that she was not handsome enough? Why should she allow herself to be vulnerable again when up against even the other women in her home city of Meryton, she'd been found wanting.

She had to get out of her head. This was most ridiculous.

"Come, Miss Elizabeth, your ghouls are disturbing even my peace of mind." Mr. Darcy held up the book and patted the chair at his side. "Whatever your demons, let Shakespeare work his magic. This sonnet is a good one..." He wiggled his eyebrows and Elizabeth relaxed. No matter her opinion of the man, she could enjoy his company. She did not have to accept his suit. She could simply sit at his side and read Shakespeare. Perform Shakespeare for the party. Who knew the others who would attend. There would be more friendships available to her, presumably.

She eyed Mary again. And Elizabeth felt it worth the effort to stay and to participate if only for dear Mary who might not have another chance such as this again.

Her head dipped in acceptance. "I am being a bit of a torrent, am I not?"

"A cyclone of the smallest, most docile kind." He grinned. "But are we not all that way sometimes?"

"I don't know. It is a new sensation for me. I do think this will help." She sat close. They placed the book between them. And Mr. Darcy grinned. "I think you will see what I see in this sonnet? It lends itself to a most diverting read, indeed."

Elizabeth could be polite, but she determined then and there she would not be allowing the charming side to the double personality of Mr. Darcy to break down her defenses because who knew when the rude and prideful version would make an appearance and she fall short in his eyes once again.

CHAPTER 6
ARTHUR DARCY

Arthur didn't know what to do with the skittish Miss Elizabeth. One minute he had barely warmed up her hesitancy and then the next without warning she was back to the cold bristly suspicious version he'd first met. Perhaps there was not more to her to know. Perhaps she was merely dealing with too much to accept kindness and caring into her life? He determined to be as gentle with her as possible but to look elsewhere for relationships at the party. Perhaps there was yet one who would be the warm-hearted woman he desired to have at his side. This house party was certainly not his last hope, but it would be helpful to find such a woman now and grow in their relationship over the course of the season as opposed to attempting yet again to find her in London amidst all the posturing and falsity that existed there.

They had retired for the evening in preparation for dinner at which Lord Shackley expected the rest of the guests. Darcy's valet had already helped him dress, brushed down his dinner coat and spent an overly large amount of time to fix his hair to perfection, much to his consternation. Darcy stepped outside his bedroom to see Miss Elizabeth and Miss Mary exiting theirs as well, though at the opposite end of the hall.

They looked lovely. There was something extra rosy about Miss Mary. He smiled to himself. Perhaps there was already an interest for her? He hoped so. She seemed rather lovely, if awkward and perhaps unsure. And she seemed to deserve good things. Though he wasn't certain Lord Perceval provided. He frowned.

And then Miss Elizabeth gasped and turned from him.

He'd been looking in their direction still with the frown on his face. He quickly replaced it with a more placid and engaging expression, but it was too late. Miss Elizabeth whispered to Miss Mary, and they both hurried off toward the stairs at the other end of the hall. So much reaction from a frown on his face. Though he supposed it wasn't pleasant to feel as though a man was frowning at you. She'd frowned at him on several occasions.

He arrived down in the sitting room outside the dining room to gather for dinner. Many more of the guests had also arrived and he had a moment of his earlier boyhood nerves. His chest tightened and the air around him became more difficult to breathe.

Miss Elizabeth shared a glance with him, a flash of concern perhaps for him gave him a dose of courage. But she looked away as quickly and he wondered if he'd imagined her sudden empathy. How could she even know how he felt from so far away?

The footman announced, "Mr. Arthur Darcy of Pemberley."

The room grew quiet and as he always dreaded, many eyes turned to him. But the women did not have the typical mercenary gleam. Perhaps they were outside of the London crowd enough to have not heard of Pemberley?

One woman stepped up immediately. Their host stood at her side though he seemed somewhat reluctant. Darcy found that amusing. "Lord Shackley. You have what promises to be a diverting house party."

"Thank you. Yes, it all begins, doesn't it?"

The woman at his right cleared her throat.

"Might I present Miss Lilly? She hails from a small borough almost to Brighton."

She curtseyed deep and low and fluttered her eyelashes.

He did not see the appeal of the eyelash fluttering. But he knew it to be a sign that she was interested enough to attract his attention. So he reached for her hand and bowed over it. "And I'm Mr. Darcy. It's a pleasure to meet you."

Her other hand immediately went to fluttering about at her chest, another thing women often did. And what did that fluttering mean? Was she nervous? Scared? Happy?

Her giggles seemed to indicate happiness.

But the fluttering. Her expression looked more ill at ease than anything.

"The pleasure is mine, certainly. To think I'd meet someone from Derbyshire. I never thought to ever even leave our small situation, perhaps a season in Brighton, maybe Bath, but never... She put a hand on her mouth. "I talk too much. I already know I do. I shall attempt to pretend that this is all normal for me, that I see great lords of grand estates every day." She swallowed, though it seemed difficult. "Forgive me." Her face burned a beet-red and sweat formed on her brow.

He reached for his handkerchief. "Be at ease, Miss Lilly. We seem a friendly enough group. Lord Shackley would not have the other sorts in his home, I'd imagine."

She nodded. "Thank you." She dabbed her face with his handkerchief and was about to hand it back but Lord Shackley cleared his throat and when she caught his gaze, he shook his head.

So she tucked it in a small reticule she had hanging at her wrist. "I just don't know how I'll remember to stop talking. I get started when I'm nervous. And Mama always says the other people need a chance. And she also says that a man doesn't really want to hear all the things in my head. He only wants to know a few. He mostly wants to tell me what's in his head. And…" She sighed. "And there I go again."

Darcy became a bit more charmed. Here was an innocent creature. He'd thought her mercenary but truly she didn't have any experience at all in Society, that he could see. "Perhaps you should just be yourself. Mamas mean well, but sometimes they might make things more difficult than they need to be."

She nodded and seemed to bite back whatever might be itching to come pouring forth. He laughed to himself. "Shall we meet some others?" He indicated that Lord Shackley should lead the way, and he held his arm for Miss Lilly to take. She sucked in her breath and fluttered a bit more but to her credit, said nothing. Her nod was almost regal as she placed her hand on his arm. Her innocence was refreshing after the expert manipulations of many of the women he came in contact with.

They turned to a man at Darcy's left. "This is Lord Devering; comes from an estate in the far north of England, if you can believe it. We are fortunate he would travel so far."

He nodded.

"This is Mr. Darcy and Miss Lilly."

Darcy held out his hand. The man shook it briefly, his face hardly evoking more than a slight tremor in his lips that might have become a smile if he were to nurture the motion a bit more.

Miss Lilly giggled again. "A lord. Goodness." Her mumbling was perhaps not heard by the noble in question but Mr. Darcy's eyes lit with amusement.

To his credit, Lord Devering did kiss the proffered hand and bowed smartly.

Miss Lilly and Lord Devering commenced some form of conversation. Miss Elizabeth was surrounded. Joint laughter sounded and her face beamed.

He was enchanted yet again. If only to have such happiness directed at him. What would it take to win over her appreciation? Was it worth the effort? What if she were the type of woman to be pleasant when necessary but behind the closed doors of any home, she would be tiresome at best. She just didn't seem like the type to play harpy at home. Not with such expressive eyes, not with such a ready laugh. Nothing about her was forced. He could appreciate her sincerity, certainly, even if it meant seeing a less pleasant side to herself.

He shook himself back to Miss Lilly's nervous laugh. He could not be talking himself into pursuing a woman who was obviously not interested and was perhaps not even a nice person.

Miss Lilly was looking at him with wide expectant eyes.

"I apologize. A bit of woolgathering as I consider this very intriguing group."

"Lord Devering was asking me about London."

"Ah, I have been often. What would you like to know?"

Miss Elizabeth's gaze from across the room fell on him. He felt it as a pleasant tingling sensation travelled to his chest. He caught her gaze and held it a moment. She had no less than three men vying for her attention, one actively telling her something. But the room quieted, and he suddenly wished more than anything to simply be at her side, that they could have a quiet corner and that the others would be less interested in her and more in each other.

He reluctantly dragged his attention back to his two companions. "I find London to be most enjoyable in the smaller seasons. I try to avoid the peak of the main season myself. But I can see how it might be preferable to others."

Lord Devering nodded. "I, of course, must travel to London for the peak of the Season as Parliament is in session."

Darcy smiled. "Too true. Excellent reminder. The very reason for the Season technically, is it not? All the families coming in with the lords to participate in Parliament?"

"I once heard of a miss in a neighboring town who went for the London Season. She had a sponsor in an aunt, and she was married that very season. To a lord." Her eyes were wide in wonder at the notion, and then she swallowed as her face turned pink. "And you're a lord as well. I must seem such a bumpkin to you both."

Lord Devering then did a surprising thing. His eyes turned tender and he placed her hand in the crook of his arm. "I find you to be quite pleasant, refreshing."

Darcy's eyes widened but he nodded in approval. Excellent.

Lord Shackley, who had moved slightly to

his left to participate in another conversation winked at him.

And that left Darcy to himself for a moment. He gravitated to the table with lemonade—which happened to be closer to Miss Elizabeth.

She cleared her throat as though it might be dry? He hoped. He hurried to the table, snatched up two lemonades and then approached her side.

None of the other men had noticed or thought to offer a beverage yet. Their loss. She stepped to the side to make space for him as if she knew he was coming. Gratified, he held out the cup. "I thought you might like a lemonade, Miss Elizabeth."

Her smile brightened her face and was for once directed fully and solely at him. "I do indeed feel parched. Thank you." She sipped the drink. "Much better."

He did not quite preen, but he felt the victory of such a gallant delivery inside his chest from his head down to his toes.

Miss Elizabeth did the honors, and he was soon introduced to two new lords and a gentleman, all from Kensington area near his aunt's estate, Rosings. But everything they said faded in his mind as soon as Miss Elizabeth moved closer to him. She did not quite place a hand on his arm, but she did turn to him as though they were together.

Interesting.

One of the men laughed overly loud. Was he talking of hunting?

Miss Elizabeth's attention had drifted, and though he too wished to know more of the grouse available on Lord Shackley's estate, he could see it was not a topic of interest to the ladies present. He held out his arm. "Might I beg a bit of your time with a turn about the room?"

Her grateful expression was reward enough. He decided that not only did he wish to see her smiling eyes but also the appreciative gleam again directed at him. This congenial side to Miss Elizabeth was almost enough for him to forget the disturbing and unhappy version that sometimes showed itself.

As soon as they were out of earshot, she squeezed his arm with her fingers. "Thank you. I did not know how to extricate myself. I think after many minutes of such discussion I had nothing more to add." She shook her head. "And they were talking of me accompanying to hold their kills." She wrinkled her nose. "I don't know much about the ladies of the *Ton*, but do they really enjoy such an activity? And would they wish to accompany a man to watch him shoot birds and then hold them for him?"

Darcy snorted. "I could never imagine you doing such a thing. Why worry about what other women do?"

"I do not often concern myself but now I am curious."

He thought for a moment. "I daresay there would be some who would do just about anything if they thought it would win them a man." He chose his words carefully. "But at what cost?"

"What do you mean?"

"Well, why attempt to win someone with false pretenses? Is not the goal to find compatibility? Would she then keep up her ruse for the rest of her life? Hardly not."

Miss Elizabeth's smile grew into a knowing grin. "I sense a sore subject."

He had to laugh to himself. "Yes. I do admit to a fear of marrying a complete stranger only to discover she is not the woman I at least hoped she might be."

"How can one truly come to know another, though? There will be some elements of surprise in a marriage, I would presume."

"Certainly. But it is my hope they will only be the good kinds of surprises."

She tapped her lips with one finger and Darcy could not help but study her mouth. It was full and pink and soft. His own went dry. What would it be like to kiss such a mouth? To kiss such a woman? He almost laughed out loud. She'd never allow it. He'd seen the side to her that might push him away if he dared to try.

"Are you listening to me?" She frowned.

"I am... I was. But I was distracted. Please repeat just the last bit?" He widened his eyes with his most innocent-looking smile.

"Oh, fine. Are you with me this time?"

"Yes, riveted."

She toyed with one of her ringlets and then began again. The curl tickled her face in just the right way and bounced back when she released it.

But he focused on her words.

"What I am trying to say is important. There will of course be unpleasant surprises. But they might seem less so if you really love your wife?"

JEN GEIGLE JOHNSON

Then she colored prettily. "With you looking at me so intently I realize suddenly that our conversation is of a more intimate nature."

"I quite enjoy it and you. If people are not willing to broach such topics, how can we ever truly come to know another?"

"I suppose it is exactly what you are trying to say, isn't it? That we should connect better?"

"Yes, precisely. Now tell me what sorts of surprises would be palatable and which ones would not be pleasant no matter how much you know a person?"

Her lips pursed and he tried not to notice but they made a delicious-looking little pout that he found hard to resist in his thoughts.

"I think I should not abide a man who sleeps in nor one who slurps his tea."

He nearly choked on his surprise. "Pardon me? Slurps?"

"Yes, surely no one slurps in polite company, but does he slurp when he thinks he's alone? Would he slurp when we are so comfortable with one another that we relax into personal habits?"

He considered her a moment. And then he laughed. "And slurping? That's the thing? That's the personal habit you might not be able to abide?"

Her mouth twitched. "Well, and other things men might do of which I am unaware. But yes. And sleeps in, don't forget."

"Not even on a lazy Sunday?"

"I suppose after a ball, one might sleep the day away. But on most days, I should most enjoy a person who wishes to be outside with me, exploring or walking or riding or...I don't know; when the sun is up I feel this call to welcome it, to feel it." Her speech picked up and her words started racing out of her. "And even the rain. To feel it on my face is delicious. How could a bed hold a person when such a glorious earth is available just outside the door?" Her eyes shone with passion.

"I don't know. You are absolutely correct and I shall never waste my opportunities in something so paltry as my bed ever again."

She nodded. "Just so." Then she turned to him. "I know we are partly in jest, but a serious answer to your question would simply be to run from unkindness. If you are both attempting to be good to the other, if your inner soul is kind, then I think you can make any relationship work."

He was quiet, considering the profundity of her words, perhaps for too long because she began to fidget and then said, "But I can't believe all that I just said in a few breaths only. You must have hit upon an important topic to me." She didn't meet his eyes. "Perhaps you could share your thoughts now as well? What might be an unhappy surprise for you?"

"I think you have expressed exactly my feelings. Find a person who is inherently kind and is willing to try." He rested a hand over the top of hers. He'd never had such a conversation with a woman at a social event before. He felt changed for the better. And a new desire to ensure his own kindness grew in him.

"And how do you feel about pride, Mr. Darcy?" Her expression turned calculating. "And about dancing at small assemblies? Do you feel any woman might be beneath you?"

Something about her expression very obviously had drifted from the teasing congenial tone to one of almost accusation. He felt suddenly very much like he was being trapped. By what, he could not fathom.

"I—"

Lord Shackley's footman opened the doors to the dining room just then, and he began calling them in to dinner.

"Would you join me?" He smiled down at a once again distant-looking Miss Elizabeth but she nodded. "I would be honored."

CHAPTER 7
ELIZABETH

Every time Elizabeth thought she was getting to know the real Mr. Darcy, the memory of his own unkindness returned. And she perhaps should not have ruined their moment, but how could they openly discuss being kind to others when he had been unkind in his thoughts and conversation about her? Even if he didn't know she heard him, his words, his thoughts about her had not been kind or kindly directed. And he had yet to even mention their time at the assembly in Meryton. Could he not remember her at all? How could she believe him to be truly interested in her if she was so completely forgettable by him?

It was too much to understand. But she

could not forget. She would not let herself forget because of the very conversation they had just had. It was so easy to pretend to be any manner of person. And she had seen a side to Mr. Darcy that would certainly be an unpleasant surprise.

Though she entered with Mr. Darcy, they were not seated together. Instead she was near Lord Shackley at the head of the table to his right and across from a lovely man who had not been present until the very call to dinner: the vicar, a Mr. Miller. To her right sat one of the lords so intent on discussing the hunt, Lord Smathering. Mr. Darcy sat way down at the other end of the table near Mary and Lord Perceval. He did not look overly pleased, while Mary and Lord Perceval seemed to be chattering away as though catching up like old friends.

What a lovely turn for her dear sister. Perhaps something wonderful could happen for her as well as Jane. Elizabeth might have to wait. Though there were some she had not conversed with yet at this party.

At the table, six pairs had begun their first course. Everyone there was interesting in their own right and quite handsome or lovely as the case allowed. The vicar and Lord Shackley were a pair she guessed; otherwise the numbers were even, and the party was well planned. She would give her compliments to the housekeeper who had likely done the brunt of all the work to create such an event.

She had not met many of the women. Miss Lilly, a lovely woman from outside of Brighton, seemed fresh from home with very little worldly experience. She sat at Mary's other side. Elizabeth was pleased to see that as well. Every woman needed another who could be trusted. And something about Lilly was all about innocence. Elizabeth would be surprised to see even a drop of guile in her. But then there were a few women in the middle of the table with intelligent expressions and narrow eyes who seemed to be more of the calculating and managing types, the kind who had already matched everyone at the table in the most advantageous of ways for their own benefit. Of course Elizabeth did not know as much about them yet, but they had a certain air of condescension and omniscience that Elizabeth would as soon avoid if possible.

One of those three looked at Mr. Darcy more than any other person in the room, but he had as yet to notice or return her gazes. Elizabeth smiled. Good luck to her winning his attention, let alone his hand.

One more woman was left to know or figure out, and Elizabeth was inclined to like her. She seemed a tiny bit older than the rest, but she sat on the other side of Lord Smathering and so Elizabeth could not hold a real conversation with her, but their gazes met enough times in reaction to the many hunting references coming from Lord Smathering that Elizabeth felt she was a kindred friend already. She heard her being referred to as Miss Vincent. She reminded Lizzie of a really nice governess; though she was beautiful in every way, she seemed to be the governess type, or at least someone who had responsibility for others. She had an air of independence and intelligence about her. Elizabeth simply felt she could learn much from her. And so she resolved that when the women separated out, she would seek out Miss Vincent.

The vicar surprised her with many very direct questions. It lent itself to an enjoyable conversation, if not a slightly embarrassing one.

"Tell me, Miss Elizabeth, are the young men of your acquaintance men of God?"

She swallowed, trying to gather her thoughts. "Without speaking ill of anyone, I will have to say I'm not certain. Mary is actually the better person to ask such a question. Who is one to say if one is a man or woman of God?" She sipped her drink, attempting to wet her lips. "Such things can easily be hidden, can they not?"

He dipped his head in acknowledgement. "I quite agree. Let me rephrase my question. Are there any you feel would be a good vicar?"

At this she laughed. But at his perfectly serious expression, she smoothed her face and chose to take his question seriously. "I suppose so, yes, perhaps the Lucas' oldest son. They are a family in a neighboring town to ours. But he might be the only one. We do have a regiment stationed in Meryton at the moment."

At the mention of Meryton, Mr. Darcy's gaze flitted to her for a moment and then drifted away.

So he might remember her? What an odd thing to forget, a whole person in one's life. She couldn't fathom such a thing, not yet anyway. Perhaps as she grew older...

The vicar nodded, knowingly. "Those men in

the military are at times good candidates for a position in the clergy. They need a living often. And they have seen hardship in some cases and would have some depth and compassion for others."

"Do you feel then, that an important responsibility for a man of the cloth would be to feel that compassion? What about the need to teach your flock, to exhort them to better behavior?"

He considered her a moment and then shook his head. "I feel that the more a person is loved, the better they will behave. Teachings from the pulpit may abound, but to feel loved is a changing phenomenon indeed."

Elizabeth nodded more than was socially acceptable, but she'd never heard such a concept before and it was sinking in in ways that were working a change in her. "I do believe that is one of the most remarkable things I've yet heard. And I will admit to many a long sermon being ignored, but the vicar who came by and prayed with my mother when she first took to her nerves, was a man I would follow and listen to." She thought of his many actions with the tenants and the assistance he was to their whole village, and she resolved to pay better attention to him and to ways she might assist in their own congregation.

Mr. Miller ate his food carefully with small bites. "Are you and your sister of influence in your area?"

"My sister perhaps more than I when it comes to the flock. She finds herself studying Fordyce's sermons and visiting tenants with mini sermons of her own, I'm afraid."

The vicar's lips twitched, and he studied Mary from down the table. "Extraordinary."

Elizabeth did not share how unbearable it felt to be a recipient of one of her sister's lectures. She nodded. "She is quite remarkable and unique among women."

At length, Lord Shackley stood. "And now we invite the lovelier sex to please partake of some respite in the lavender drawing room while we take to our more uncouth pursuits here." He laughed.

The women stood and Elizabeth found her sister's arm. "Goodness, you have had quite the conversation."

Mary blushed for a moment. "He is most diverting. I think you would enjoy his humor."

"I'm certain I would if you do. Do we know anything about him?"

"What is there to know besides our complete compatibility?" She smiled a dreamy and utterly naïve smile, and Elizabeth realized her mistake in not preparing Mary for the euphoric sense of infatuation up against the cares of determining if it was a truly wise direction to follow. "Well, as a matter of fact, there are many things to know."

They entered the lavender room together and Miss Vincent joined them. "I have been wanting to know the sister of the intriguing Miss Mary." She smiled warmly and Mary introduced them. "Miss Vincent comes from the coastal town of Scarborough. She has actually been sea bathing before."

"Have you? I must know how it is done."

"I am happy to give you all the details, though some are more palatable than others." She shivered.

Elizabeth laughed. "Now I must know."

"Perhaps in less crowded company."

She nodded, more than a little intrigued.

The housekeeper, Mrs. Godly, joined them, followed by maids with trays. "We have some cordial and tea as well as some of our cook's excellent tarts and small cakes. I think you will find it all to be delectable as she is much applauded in the area."

An appreciative murmur and small exclamations of delight seemed to gratify Mrs. Godley enough. She curtseyed and left them to themselves.

"Shall I pour?" One of the ladies with calculating eyes stepped forward as acting hostess for their group. A more competitive side of Elizabeth would have bristled at that, but as things sat, she had no need to position herself in any which way. She was more of the mind of Mr. Darcy, seeking connection before posturing. Though she was rather particular about her tea. "Thank you. Shall I assist?"

The flat-lined smile sent in Elizabeth's direction was not the friendliest of reactions, but she chose to ignore it. Perhaps she simply did not know how to be friendly. Though that idea was ridiculous, it was easier to swallow and respond to as well.

Miss Vincent and Mary laughed together while Elizabeth dealt with the flat-lipped tea pourer. "I don't believe we have been introduced. I'm Elizabeth Bennet..."

The other woman sniffed and then nodded. "It is a pleasure to meet you. I'm Miss Winderly, from London."

"Oh, you are the only person here from actual London, I do believe. So many are from so far."

"I cannot account for it myself. Lord Shackley was a dear friend of my late governess."

"And of your parents?"

"Certainly, though they have much less to do with me than my governess did."

Much needed explanation in that situation in Elizabeth's mind but she let it pass. "Do you know anyone else at the party?"

"Not from before, no. How about you?"

She was about to explain Mr. Darcy's brief meeting but decided against it. "My sister. Mary Bennet." She indicated Mary.

"Ah yes, she's lovely."

"Thank you."

They poured and passed out tea to everyone's specifications and at last for themselves. They moved to sit but not before Miss Winderly poured a sizable amount of cordial into her tea.

Elizabeth wondered at that but pretended she didn't notice.

They had been offered cordial, had they not? Miss Winderly could drink of whatever she liked even if she hid it in her tea.

A shadow passed in the hall.

"Mr. Darcy!" One of the other two ladies nearly shrieked out his name.

He stepped back into the doorframe with his eyebrows up. "Yes?"

She rushed to his side and clung to his arm. "Would you care for some tea?" She nearly dragged him forward.

He paused their entrance. "I do believe I'm intruding, am I not?" His eyes sought Elizabeth, who could only shrug in general amusement.

He frowned as though she was no help. Which, in all honesty, she was too busy being entertained to assist. But as he fumbled his way forward with several excuses half-begun on his lips, she took a bit of mercy. "I think I heard that Lord Shackley plans to discuss our enjoyment with the men this evening. You do not wish Mr. Darcy to miss an opportunity to be paired with one of us."

"Oh no!" She stepped back, nearly pushing

him out. "Yes, I suppose we will all get a turn to be paired with you, no? Not simply always the same woman?" The flitting gaze that washed over Lizzie felt less than friendly. It was not her fault at all that she'd spent time with the much sought-after Mr. Darcy.

He glanced at Elizabeth then dipped his head. "I do hope to be paired with those Lord Shackley deems compatible as well as have an opportunity to know you all better."

She seemed mildly pacified by his response and turned from him as he bowed to the room in general, then with one last look at Elizabeth, exited again.

What had he been doing wandering the halls anyway?

Miss Vincent stood at her side. "I suspect Mr. Darcy would prefer your company above all others here."

She raised her eyebrows but Miss Vincent had moved away. Where had that come from?

At any rate, they had finished their tea and were growing restless before the men joined them.

Servants followed, and tables for cards were set up in different corners of the room.

Lord Shackley announced whist and chess, and soon table groups were clustered around each game.

Mary moved toward chess and Lord Perceval was about to join her, but Mr. Darcy, in a barely polite manner, slipped in the chair opposite. "Might I enjoy the pleasure of your company, Miss Mary?"

She nodded and to her credit did not fumble through her response. "It would be my pleasure. How are you at chess?"

Elizabeth tilted her head, unsure what to think about that development. She did wish for Mary to continue such a good connection with Lord Perceval. What was Mr. Darcy trying here?

CHAPTER 8

ARTHUR DARCY

T he next day, a footman delivered the mail to everyone on the back verandah. A surprising amount of people were receiving correspondence at the party. Arthur's was from Georgiana, which was to be expected. She often wrote to him no matter where he was, for which he was grateful. It had not been easy to be her guardian—not because she herself was difficult but because he didn't know the first thing about being a guardian. And now that she was mostly of age and become an interest to so many, he felt a greater responsibility. She wrote to Fitz as well, but for some reason the brunt of the harder decisions and the care fell more squarely on his shoulders. As with everything.

Miss Elizabeth also received mail; looked to be two letters. But not Miss Mary. She stood and left to the gardens, just off the steps of the verandah. When Lord Perceval moved to follow her, Darcy pocketed his letters and followed them both.

Miss Elizabeth stepped up to his side. "I can't help but wonder at your interest in the gardens at this very moment."

"Oh, I was..."

Her expression did not bode well for her reception to anything he said. She had the same suspicion he'd seen on her face earlier.

"I am offering myself as a chaperone of sorts for Miss Mary, if you must know."

"And do you not think me capable?"

"Of course you are. I would assume. Though I noticed you also received mail and might wish to peruse it in quiet. I was merely offering my services in a most unobtrusive manner. I hoped you would not notice except to think that Mary would be quite taken care of?"

Her eyes softened and she nodded. "I am

most grateful. There is an urgent nature about the hand of my sister, so I wish to see that all is well."

He dipped his head. "Please. I have this well in hand. I am quite adept at frustrating the advances of young men who would wish a bit more intimate setting with young ladies."

Miss Elizabeth watched him curiously but then nodded. "Thank you. I'll join you momentarily." She situated herself on a bench in the sun looking so at ease and so inviting he almost did not follow Miss Mary but her laughter soon motivated him to give the two a bit of company.

They grew quiet and so he picked up his pace through the gardens and at last stumbled into a walled-in garden of sorts, surrounded by hedgerows, with a fountain in the center. Miss Mary was standing close to Lord Perceval, her chin upturned, and the wastrel looked as though he was actually contemplating making the most of his opportunity.

With a not too subtle throat clearing from Darcy, Lord Perceval created some space between he and Miss Mary and offered her his arm. They murmured something together and then began a slow pace, walking side by side. Darcy made himself interested in that particular fountain and wondered about the rose arbor that he could see rising up above the hedgerow on the other side of the garden.

The fountain spread a thin mist in the air and the smell of the roses drifted to him in such a pleasant subtle way, he wished for a bit of company himself. Giggling from behind him was welcome, but when he turned there was no one in the immediate garden. They must have been walking by in another of the sequestered spaces. Lord Shackley had a beautiful situation. Arthur had something similar in Pemberley, but the whole property tended to be less structured and more wild. Which his father had preferred. But Darcy thought there might be space for a sculpture garden and some hedgerows. He corrected his thoughts. His new property would have space for something like that. He made some mental notes of what to ask the gardeners to plant.

At times Darcy was fine with leaving Pemberley. He was not the heir. He'd known that since birth. But all his efforts over the course of his life had certainly grown his attachment and

feelings about how things were done at Pemberley. And to see his brother so seldomly engaged
in any of the decision-making was of course a
concern to Arthur.

He had sent feelers out to determine if there
were any properties available for sale or even
land without any structures yet on it. Luckily his
investments had grown, and his small estate
from his mother was also profitable. There was
much he could do, and he best be about giving
greater attention to such things. A working
estate with current tenants would be the ideal
choice. And he'd enjoy being close to Pemberley,
but then would he end up running two estates,
his brother leaving all the work to him?

The idea of creating a legacy was appealing.
To think that he could begin what his ancestor
Darcy had; to gift something of worth to his
future generations that he himself had created.
His breath filled his chest along with a huge
sense of satisfaction.

A soft hand rested on his arm. Her entrance
had been so gentle, so natural that he hadn't
realized Miss Elizabeth's approach. As gently as
her entrance, he recognized that she seemed to
fit in with his plans. She matched the sense of

pride and hope for his future generations. He could not place why she seemed to so seamlessly blend in with his direction, but she did.

The eyes turned up to his face were smiling as she tipped her head toward Miss Mary. "They seem happy," she whispered.

He couldn't help but feel a touch of concern, but he nodded. "They do indeed. I haven't yet conversed with them but they have been doing enough of that on their own."

Their heads were dipped together in that moment, and Miss Mary seemed intent upon Lord Perceval's every word. Again, Darcy felt concern. What were the man's intentions? He was not Miss Mary's guardian or anything like it. But he couldn't help but notice she had no one speaking for her in that way at the party. If Lord Perceval was about a small flirtation during the party only, and she would be left picking up the pieces of her heart and hope and expecta-tions, Darcy felt he should intervene. Marked attention and then a withdrawal of such left the lady in question up for ridicule and shame. Lord Perceval, while not a rake or a cad by any stretch, had certainly shown no recent intentions of settling down. If Darcy had heard correctly, he was much sought after among the ladies of the *Ton*. Why would he leave all of that for the simpleness of Miss Mary? She was pretty enough naturally. She had a gentleness to her that Darcy admired. But she was not like any of the diamonds that Lord Perceval was reported to visit during a London Season. Had something occurred to sully his reputation there?

"You are displeased?" Miss Elizabeth's hand pressed into his forearm, and her expression filled with concern.

"No. Not...necessarily. Miss Mary looks happy." He didn't know why he hesitated to explain Lord Perceval's reputation. He should. Miss Elizabeth deserved to know. But at the same time, he believed in giving everyone second chances, new starts. If the man would allow himself a woman like Miss Mary, it could do everything for his life. Darcy believed in the power of a good well-suited marriage. He'd seen it in his parents and he craved it in his life.

"You are so distant in your thoughts. How were your letters from home?"

He turned his attention to the beautiful woman at his side. "I admit to not reading them yet. And yours?"

"The first one is so full of happiness and excitement from Jane that I can only think that things are well. The militia is there, and that is adding much energy in my younger sisters. Mother is pleased. Father is spending more time in the library." She shrugged. "I think it seems like all is well. I have such high hopes for dear Jane."

"Hopes? In what way? Jane is your elder sister is she not?"

Miss Elizabeth looked at him curiously for a moment, and he felt yet again in her presence like he was missing something rather important. But her expression cleared and she nodded. "Yes, she is elder. Although most don't know that on first meeting. She and I are so close in age."

"And you are dear friends, are you not?"

"Oh yes, she is my closest, most dear friend and confidante. I am truly blessed to have someone who cannot think ill of another, who is perpetually kind and wants my happiness almost as much as I do, sometimes even more than I do."

"I, too, have such trust in my sister. Georgiana. Though she is much younger than I, barely sixteen." He led Miss Elizabeth toward the other garden, toward the roses. He wished to see her near them, to see if she would be as entranced by the sweetness of their smell as he had been.

Lord Perceval and Miss Mary turned that direction as well.

"I feel I would learn much about you if I were to meet Georgiana." She smiled. "Are you similar?"

"We are, in many ways. But she views me more as a guardian than a sibling, I'm afraid."

"Are your parents not available?"

"Oh, no. They have both passed, unfortunately. She looks to me for that kind of direction now." He paused before bringing up his brother. There was no need to explain the difference in their personalities in this instance as it might only disparage his name, which Arthur was unwilling to do. Fitz was a good person, just not ever considered the responsible one. But Miss Elizabeth could make her own opinions of his brother were they to ever meet. "She is the sweetest, most lovely person, and I have delayed her entrance in Society because I'm not certain I can help her in the ways needed. No one will be good enough, I'm afraid." He shrugged.

But Miss Elizabeth smiled. "Oh, to have a brother like you. Though I'm not sure you'd survive all five of us Bennets out in Society at the same time." She shook her head. "And Father seems to be avoiding the immensity of that challenge. I can see why it would be too much for any person." She looked to Miss Mary. "This is so good for her. I'm afraid if not for moments like this, Mary is quite ignored."

Miss Elizabeth and Darcy walked together, closer than was necessary. Her shoulder brushed against his arm more often than not. After a moment, she brought her other hand to his arm. "This is nice. I much prefer being outside in almost any weather."

He nodded. "In that, we are in complete agreement. The last walk I took at home was in fact during a rainfall."

She laughed. "No! I have done the same."

"The servants." He shook his head.

But she laughed. "Oh, I heard about it for days, everyone thinking I'd catch my death from cold." She shrugged. "And here I am, as healthy as ever."

"Glowing." He reached over and tucked a

stray hair behind her ear. "You are lovely. Outside suits you."

She did not dip her head in modesty at the compliment but looked him full in the face. "Thank you. I must admit you surprise me. You are so different here, and so caring, attentive." She looked as though she might say more, and Darcy would like to hear it. Why would it be a surprise? But he'd met enough of the men in the *Ton* to know that he was not always a fair example of his sex.

"Perhaps outside suits me as well."

She nodded as though that explanation might suffice but probably wouldn't.

They entered the area with the rose arbor and Miss Elizabeth's soft gasp was gratifying to him. He was equally enthralled. The garden did not have only the one arbor but many, and bushes of many different colors and varieties. The air was filled with a soft sweetness. He breathed in. "My compliments to Lord Shackley's gardeners. This is remarkable."

"A work of art. Someone put their heart in here." She reached forward and ran her fingertips along the edges of the roses. "See how well they have planned and pruned each bush." She leaned forward to smell a lavender rose. "Mmm. Like a mixture of honey and lemons."

She had stepped away from him to admire the roses, and he missed her closeness acutely. How had she so quickly entwined herself in his needs? Did he need her by his side? He needed to spread out his attentions if so...or perhaps he didn't. As she walked farther long, admiring rose after rose, he could see himself happily at her side for many hours yet without wishing for a break.

She turned to him. "This one is my favorite. Have you smelled any at all? Come, you must determine a favorite."

He smiled at the game and then dutifully smelled rose after rose in her wake. When he got near to the one she deemed a favorite, he tried to guess which. There were two options, a fiery orange and a subtle lavender. As he smelled one after another she approached and leaned forward again. "What are you doing?"

"I'm guessing which is your favorite."

Her smile widened. "And? What is the verdict?"

He pointed to the orange. "While I see you are full of passion, I don't think the smell is one you would prefer to inhale like you were. I'm going to guess the softer lavender?"

She rested a hand on his arm. "You are correct. I do love the orange for its passion, but I could sleep with the lavender on my pillow and wake with it on my hair and skin and be very happy indeed." She breathed it in again, leaving Darcy with images of her lovely hair spread across a white pillow. He straightened. She was definitely doing things to him no woman had ever done.

"And can you guess mine?"

"Have you chosen?"

"I have." He crossed his arms.

"Will you not at least give me a direction? You knew the precise location of mine."

"Too true. It was back at the beginning. I have not found an equal to it yet."

She tapped her lips with one finger as he realized she was wont to do when about to toy with him. "Now we shall discover your secrets."

"My secrets?" He laughed.

"Certainly. You can tell a lot about a man by his preferred smells." She skipped ahead and called over her shoulder. "At least I assume you can." She began smelling the flowers in earnest at the entrance to their path. But it didn't take long. "This one, certainly. It's precise. Strong but not overbearing. And a touch fruity?" She cupped the rose for him to see.

"Fruity?" He shook his head. "I'm not certain fruity says much about me as a man." His frown must have shown because Miss Elizabeth laughed.

"I did not smell fruit in that. But you are correct about the rose in question. That is my favorite." He lifted her fingers in his hand and bowed to press his lips to the back of her hand. "Uncannily guessed." He placed her hand back in the crook of his arm, hoping she'd stay closer now.

"I'm quite enjoying myself, you know." Her side grin in his direction caused all kinds of interesting thumpings of his heart. He hadn't been sure up to this moment the precise location of that vital organ but now there was no mistaking it, nor its happiness at the nearness of Miss Elizabeth.

"I'm pleased to hear it, as I've made it a personal goal to please you in any manner possible."

"A personal goal? And when did you make this goal?"

"Right now." He laughed. "When I saw your smile." He lifted her hand to his lips again, keeping her as close as possible. "I would give a lot to keep that beauty permanently directed at me." He tried to express his earnestness, hoped she would know he wasn't merely saying pretty words.

She studied him for a long moment, her eyes deep windows to her hope and slight misgiving, but after a moment she nodded. "I would find your attempts welcome indeed."

The air between them felt heavy with possibility. She gazed up into his face and somehow they were closer than moments earlier, her chin lifted, her eyes full of curiosity. He peeked a glance at her lips and their softness was nearly his undoing. "Miss Elizabeth...I—"

A jarring and somewhat insolent voice called out to them, "Come now, Darcy, you must help us decide." Lord Perceval, with a wicked revenge-filled gleam in his eye, approached with Miss Mary on his arm.

Touché. Darcy supposed he deserved the interruption since he'd done the same to Lord

Perceval just minutes earlier. But he didn't like it any better for knowing he might deserve it. And his intentions with Miss Elizabeth were honorable. He was not toying with her simply because she was present. He paused. Was he? Did he wish to pursue her in a more permanent manner? He supposed he did. The more he knew her, the more he was inclined. But of course he had no way of knowing what he wanted to do about the rest of his life. Based on his current knowledge, a closeness to her, a more intimate conversation—and he had to admit even a kiss —was on his mind. How could it not be, with her entirely too tempting of a mouth so close? His cravat suddenly felt too tight, his jacket stretched across his shoulders unnaturally, and the area around him too confined. He wished for space and some distance between him and any other person.

Only he was close to them all, most particularly Miss Elizabeth.

She must have sensed something off in him because she removed her hand and stepped over to Miss Mary, linking arms with her. They began a low, out of earshot conversation, causing frowns on both men's faces.

Darcy would have laughed if he wasn't still in need of air, more air, far away from other people kinds of air. Miss Elizabeth had a much greater hold on him than he realized. With a lift of her eyelashes, he was at her command. He'd almost kissed the woman. He'd certainly shown his desire to do so. If he could just have a moment to think...

CHAPTER 9
ELIZABETH

Elizabeth showed Mary her letter. "There are bits in here for you as well, plus I haven't yet read our second letter." She pointed to the other side of the garden. "Shall we?"

Mary glanced at Lord Perceval for the briefest moment, but he was not paying attention, distracted by something Mr. Darcy was saying or doing, and so she nodded. "Yes, let's."

Elizabeth led them both toward two sets of benches up against a hedgerow. They sat on the first, the stone warm through their dresses, the sun soft and gentle, the breeze light and filled with the scents of roses and soft earth. Now and again, hints of mist from the fountain drifted over on the wind.

She risked a smile at Mr. Darcy. He was watching her, only half an ear to the lord at his side.

What had just almost happened? Heat filled her chest, her heart rate leaping all over the place. She needed to fan her face. Would he have kissed her? She swallowed. Would she have let him? Such scandal to be crossing her mind. But even more scandalous, Elizabeth wanted him to try again. And she thought she would let him. How could she think such things? And if she were to go around kissing men, that didn't mean she was courting them or they her; didn't mean she was meant to marry them. She sucked in her breath. Was Mr. Darcy thinking of marrying her? Courting her?

He did not seem the type to pass out kisses to just anyone, and he certainly didn't seem the type to toy with a woman's emotions. He might be very seriously considering courting her. She tried to breathe normally through a still pounding heart and with shaking hands. Hopefully to Mr. Darcy and anyone else glancing her way, she was calmly listening to the fountain even though her insides raged in a torrent like she'd never felt before.

It was certainly not like him to toy with a woman, was it?

She tried to swallow back the lump in her throat and calm the rapidity of her breathing. Remembering her other letter, she broke the seal. Anything to distract her at this moment would be a saving grace.

She fanned her face a moment and then lowered her gaze to the latest news from home.

My dear Lizzie,

I have news of the most distressing nature though I can hardly believe it myself. I am left without knowing how to move on, my dear sister, so surprised and in an upheaval. Mama hardly knows how to leave her bed, her smelling salts not aiding in their typical restorations. Father has confined himself to the study and Lydia is heaven only knows where, for she is not at home and no one seems to be aware of her any longer.

Elizabeth clutched the papers, her eyes reading as quickly as she could, though trying not to miss a single word so as not to misunderstand.

Mr. Bingley has left the area with not a word to

me. I received the smallest note from his sister, directing me that he would soon be joining her and Mr. Darcy's sister whom she most dearly hopes to call sister herself soon. Oh Lizzie, I can scarce write the words. Please. What shall I do? Advise me quickly, for I'm most desperately despondent like I've never felt. He did love me, did he not? Can I be so naïve as to have imagined his affections? Was I so wrong in his character? Could he be capable of such a deception? I need your voice or at least your words to guide me. Write swiftly.

And then included with that letter was another sheet, tucked behind. It fell out and Lizzie opened it.

And now I must tell you news that you shall not believe but I assure you I am in earnest. Lydia has run off, we believe, with an officer, one who appeared to be most charming to all but is in fact a man of great debt and poor reputation. There is no hope for any of us or wherewithal to find her. Uncle is aiding us as they are believed to be in London. But now I must beg you to come at your earliest convenience. Nothing can come of the house party at any rate. The minute someone learns of her indiscretion we are all ruined. Mary must be told gently. I'm afraid she will be most disappointed in her sister.

And about Bingley, I'm afraid to say, I'm as sad as ever but the situation with Lydia has made any hope for Bingley impossible even though he was influenced by his friend, Mr. Darcy. I had hoped that perhaps he could be convinced, that he would remember and return. The opinion of one friend cannot have such a strong effect. But now it does not matter. Were he to come to his senses, we could not be together, for no man should have to bear the shame of our family's guilt.

Yours etc.

Lizzie hardly knew what to think. She clutched her breast, the letters crumbled in her other hand.

"Lizzie. What is it?" Mary's voice at her side sounded miles away. She clutched her arm and with a little shake said again, "Lizzie."

At length she turned to Mary. "It is news of the worst kind. But come. We must keep it hidden as long as possible."

The horror of Lydia's situation descended on her like a weight. But the words "influenced by Mr. Darcy" crashed around in her brain, wreaking havoc on her ability to reason or even respond to Mary.

She sought him out. He was standing with

Lord Perceval in deep conversation. They both glanced in her direction enough that she suspected the topic of their conversation. And then she became suspicious of all his interactions regarding them. Why had he been the one to gallantly offer himself as chaperone? Why was he taking such an active interest? If he'd ruined Jane's relationship with Bingley, was he trying to do the same here with Mary? Her heart chilled and all warmth for him turned to a great well of hurt and anger. How could he do such a thing? Why meddle? And why toy with her heart? Surely a man that would try to ruin the happiness of not one but two beloved sisters did not actually hope to court and please her? She shook her head.

Mr. Darcy lifted his eyebrows in question and Lizzie realized he must think she was trying to communicate. She looked away, barely able to contain herself.

He dipped his head to Lord Perceval and began his approach.

"No, no no no no." Lizzie grabbed Mary's arm. "We must leave. Now."

Mary stepped forward, jerked up by Lizzie's hand. But before they could step away from the bench, Mr. Darcy was standing in front of them. "Are you well?" His eyes were tender, his voice gentle and for a moment, Lizzie glanced at his lips. He seemed so sincere, so caring. What a creton. How could he be so clever in his disguise? So gifted in his duplicity?

She shook her head, lifting her chin defiantly. "We are not well. We've received most distressing news and will be leaving the party directly." She looked away.

"Oh dear. This news. It is most distressing for me, certainly if you plan to leave. What can I do? Shall I call for the carriage?" He turned as though he would do just such a thing but Lizzie shook her head and called out. "You shall not."

"Pardon me." He tipped his head to the side.

"You have done more than enough already." She could barely be civil, her words coming out as near whispers. All the emotion suddenly caught in her throat and the sharpness of knives dug into the large lump that formed. "We shall be far better off alone." She reached for Mary but the girl did not know how to make a quick exit and seemed frozen in confusion at Elizabeth's rapid change of loyalty. Lizzie couldn't blame her, but now was the time for haste.

Mr. Darcy seemed oblivious to the severity of her distress or her disinclination to allow him to be involved at all. "Come, Miss Elizabeth. Allow me to be of assistance. If I might even know the nature of your distress, I could perhaps come to your aid?"

Lizzie stood taller, words forming and exiting her mouth without thought. "You who have been the means of destroying Jane's happiness? You? No. I don't need anything from you. Though it shall all come out at some point. I might as well say it here, so as to avoid further spread of falsehood. The facts as we know them are thus. My sister Lydia has run off with a soldier who was stationed in Meryton."

Mary gasped and clutched Lizzie's arm. She immediately regretted the callous nature in which she was blurting out the news, but she trudged on.

"She is as silly as any, I admit, but this is very unlike her. We fear the worst. She can have nothing to offer him and no enticements for them to actually marry." There, she'd said it. Her chest heaved in her breaths as though each one painful. "And so I must return home to support

Jane who is also suffering from her own broken heart."

"What? Oh dear!" Mary's eyes were full of sadness, and Lizzie could only nod.

But Mr. Darcy seemed confused and deeply troubled. "I am most distressed on your behalf and on the loss of your company. I will do what I can." He waved a hand. "Please summon a carriage and alert Lord Shackley of their immediate need to depart." He started to pace. "Distressing news indeed. What is to be done?" He paused. "Has anyone gone after them?"

"Yes of course. And I don't have further news." She pulled Mary firmly with her and headed for the house. "If you'll excuse me."

Mr. Darcy bowed. "Of course."

Lizzie paused, watching his face before turning from him, half hoping despite her hurt at his actions that he might give some semblance of hope, some inkling that all was not lost for her family. But those were all the words he had left for her. His own silence, his mouth pressed into a thin line, his inability to look her in the face, was enough to tell Elizabeth all she needed about her potential reception in any polite homes or with any well-to-do families.

Her family's fate was secure. They'd all best be looking carefully and quickly for employment. Even a governess position would be a stretch if news of their defamation were to reach many ears. She didn't look back even though she knew it was the last she was ever going to see of Mr. Darcy. He was probably counting himself and his friend lucky that he'd separated Jane from Bingley. Tears stung her eyes, but she didn't raise a hand to wipe them. Mary said nothing as they hurried as quickly as they could out of the gardens and out of sight of Mr. Darcy.

CHAPTER 10
ARTHUR DARCY

Darcy's heart sank as Miss Elizabeth hurried from him, acting as though he was the last person she wanted to witness her pain. Her circumstances were dire indeed. Women rarely recovered from such a scandal were it to ever be known. Well did he know, having just saved his own sister from an almost scandal. The evil smirk on Mr. Wickham's face, her would-be elopement fiancé, came to his mind and brought such distaste he could scarce hide his expression.

Lord Perceval stepped closer. "They'll not be welcome in most circles as soon as this gets out. It's a shame we're at the same party; perhaps tarnished ourselves." Lord Perceval sneered.

Darcy whipped around to face him. "Do not mistake my silence for any lack of support for the Bennet sisters. You would do best to never repeat a word of Miss Elizabeth's plight to another soul." He stared at the pompous lord until he nodded, once.

"It is not our business, nor should it be the topic of anyone else's." He waited until Lord Perceval nodded again. "With any luck this will blow over with no one the wiser."

The man snorted, but when Darcy paused again, he shrugged. "You can be certain I won't forget. Miss Mary and her smiles will have to find company elsewhere."

"Then you will miss the company of one of the truly special ladies of our acquaintance."

Lord Perceval sniffed but drifted away slowly until Darcy heard him call out to one of the other ladies of the party.

Darcy himself had no desire to linger any more at this house party. His mind was whirling with thoughts and his heart was in anguish for Miss Elizabeth's situation. How could he be of assistance? What was being done? These things were handled with money and influence—both of which he had. And if he could do something, anything to erase the anguish from Miss Elizabeth's face or the nervous clenching of her hands, he would do it, without question.

He hung his head as he made his way back to the house. A part of him feared, dreaded, that his involvement would distance him so far from Miss Elizabeth's good graces, that the feeling of being beholden to him would negate any chances he could ever have to further a romance with the woman. By assisting her and aiding her reputation, he would be sealing his fate to never be in her life.

Her expression as she hurried from him, her distaste in his presence, her reluctance to explain all or to accept his help were all evidence that Darcy could well have lost her forever. Her words replayed themselves. And the part about him destroying the happiness of her sister made no sense to him. He could not imagine their source, but assumed them to be spoken in a jumble, perhaps in error. He would have to explore that issue later.

His instructions to the valet were clipped but the good servant moved forward, packing his things without question. His explanations to Lord Shackley were also vague.

He clapped Darcy on the back. "We will miss you, old friend. But perhaps the assistance has been made? I understand the Misses Bennet have also left this afternoon." He watched Darcy's face, but he kept a blank expression.

"Your party has been a lovely opportunity to meet so many wonderful new faces, the people from the country who I have long wanted to know. I thank you for that."

Lord Shackley nodded, clapped him on the back again, but his eyes took on a hint of sorrow. "I did so hope that you and Miss Elizabeth would be able to come to some kind of arrangement." He shook his head. "Two finer people I have never met." He leaned back against his desk. "When I see you together, there is such a—"

"Yes, thank you. You have given us an excellent start, certainly. I have greatly enjoyed her attention."

Lord Shackley hesitated and then simply nodded in response.

Back in his room, Darcy regretted his abrupt tone to a good friend of his father, but there was no sense in raising the man's hopes or in encouraging his chatter to others about he and Miss Elizabeth Bennet.

Without much further delay, he was packed into his carriage and heading away from Lord Shackley's estate.

His time with Miss Elizabeth was enlightening, certainly, and heartbreakingly enticing. She had beguiled him, heart and soul, in the short time he'd known her. Even her confusing moods, even her frowns, her uncertainty about him. She had been so increasingly important to him, such a goal for him to reach, a conquest of sorts that he wasn't certain what to do when not in her presence. She had lit in him an intensity he'd not felt before. He could not leave her to this fate. He had resources. He had experience. And he was going to at least make certain Miss Elizabeth's situation was improved.

With very little further thought, he rapped on the ceiling. When the driver opened up the small hatch so that he could see the man's eyes, Darcy hesitated one moment only and then called out to him. "Change direction, man. We are off to London."

As soon as his trunk entered the London townhome, he sent a servant after the Bow Street Runner who had helped him with his sister. If something was amiss in London with *le bon ton*, this man would know or discover it. Hopefully he would be as aware of the gentry typically outside of London. He could only try.

Only after he was situated in his study, waiting for news with the first bit of comfortable quiet since the news Miss Elizabeth blurted out to him, did he recall her words, "You who have been the means of destroying the happiness of a much beloved sister..."

He rubbed his forehead with thumb and forefinger. How had he ruined her happiness? She mentioned Jane, but he didn't know Miss Jane. Miss Mary's? He could not imagine to what she was referring. But it seemed as though she believed her own words and that her anger over his ruining of happiness was clouding all other thoughts about him. He tapped his fingers on the desk. How could he have done such a thing? He'd stood closer to Miss Mary than was probably expected of his relationship to the family, but he'd been encouraging. He'd been helpful even. Or so he assumed. Perhaps he'd been too accommodating? Did Miss Elizabeth not want Lord Perceval in her sister's life? No, those thoughts were nonsensical. He had done nothing wrong and certainly nothing to ruin a life. He didn't know what to make of it. But perhaps it also explained her thoughts about him, her seeming predisposition to dislike him. She was of the opinion that he had ruined her sister's life.

A servant knocked and then stepped in when called for. "A Mr. Hopper to see you."

If possible, the man looked darker than the last time Darcy had seen him. But underneath the low-lying hat and the shaggy hair, his eyes twinkled with an intelligence and goodness that remained the same. Darcy trusted him implicitly. And he was the best in his trade. If anyone could find Lydia Bennet, it was Mr. Earl Hopper.

Many hours passed, during which Darcy did little besides pace the floors and ponder words he could never say to Miss Elizabeth before Mr. Hopper returned to his study with a name. "I know who the man is. None other than George Wickham."

Darcy shot to his feet with a litany of instructions, but Mr. Hopper just nodded.

"Remember sir, I've been down this road before too. I suspect we will have the cad in hand before the sun is up." He straightened his hat. "But I also expect we'll be needing to move ourselves to Brighton."

CHAPTER II
FITZWILLIAM DARCY

Netherfield had become insufferable. Bingley could do nothing but mope about, and his sister Caroline's gloat was nearly as loathsome. He had at last convinced the whole party to depart but they were now insisting to travel home with him instead of to their own places of abode. "Pemberley has the only cure for what ails us all."

He'd agreed to wait and depart with them all together, but he'd insisted that he himself was not traveling home to Pemberley just yet, so there was no need for anyone else to go.

If Fitz went to Pemberley this time of year, Arthur was certain to task him with all the responsibilities that were his.

Fitz knew they were his.

But Arthur did them so abominably well and Fitz hated them, so why should he concern himself just yet? There would be plenty of time to settle down and run the estate when he married.

And since Arthur seemed as yet in no hurry to marry or move to his own properties, Fitz was content to let his brother continue the lion share of estate running. The servants liked him better. Their steward liked him better, and Fitz suspected that even their father had liked him better. But who could blame the world? Arthur came packaged as a responsible, likable, diligent and boring person.

Fitz smirked. The people of Meryton might have thought him the same. But he couldn't possibly have danced with any of them, the lovely Elizabeth Bennet included. Her tongue and her temper sat wrong with him. She'd likely call him out for this behavior or that. She had a way of looking at a man and demanding more of him. And he, Fitz, was not ready to give more.

She'd obviously somehow heard his *handsome enough* comment. He could tell by her reaction to him. It was a shame. He had no intentions of insulting people. But he'd grown tired of Bingley fussing at him. If his friend wished to enter in the good graces of the Bennet family, then so be it. Fitz would not be following suit.

And then that family turned out to be altogether too difficult in every way. Bingley had been blind to it, but they were all so irreparably socially damaging that he'd had to step in. And when Miss Jane herself didn't look enamored, he felt duty bound to warn him off of a disastrous situation.

Who would want a mother-in-law boisterously caterwauling all day about his wealth, his children, his business, to anyone who would listen? And then discover that one's wife was not in love after all. Fitz had shaken his head and then gone about convincing Bingley that Miss Jane did not love him.

Any possible guilt was sufficiently assuaged with the ease of the convincing. No man truly besotted could possibly be dissuaded so easily. He would move on to the next pretty face and Fitz would at last be free of the place.

Theoretically.

But alas, they were not yet free. They were waiting on Caroline and some tiff with her maid.

Darcy checked his pocket watch again. It was hard to believe Caroline and Charles Bingley were related. He was all smiles and goodness, and she? Darcy shuddered a moment. Her smiles were either tight and hinted of disapproval or leery and opportunistic. Hearing her shrill voice shriek instructions to the maid forced Darcy out of doors. His trunk was already atop the carriage. He wandered to the end of the lane at the entrance to Netherfield. It really was a lovely location; wonderful property, well situated. And the house was perfect for Charles. It was an excellent first estate for him. If not for Jane and the Bennets, Charles could have been very happy there.

Horse hooves sounded from down the lane. Fitz wasn't really looking forward to seeing anyone, particularly not anyone local, but there was nothing for it. He could not very well escape except by running to the carriage and diving inside.

But it looked to be a man, riding his horse at breakneck speed. But as he drew closer to

Netherfield gates, he eased back on the pace and came to a stop in front of Fitz.

"I'm looking for Mr. Fitzwilliam Darcy."

Fitz recovered from the surprise enough to reach out a hand with some coin for the express rider. "I am Mr. Darcy. Thank you." He untied the scroll. "Do you wait for a response?"

He nodded. "Aye, sir."

Fitz made a quick work of his brother's short missive. *"I'm in London, looking for that creton, Wickham. He's done more damage than we should have allowed, now absconded with a local girl from outside of Meryton. Please do your best to pick up any trail he may have left in the area and also discover his debts, as I'm certain he has them."*

Fitz frowned.

"And then off to our aunt's, please. I am entangled in this mess until its conclusion, and our aunt is requiring attention. Please send the rider back with your response."

He eyed the man waiting on the horse. "Can you remember a short answer?"

"Yes, sir."

"Tell my brother I will do as he asks, and I await his company at Rosings Park."

The man nodded.

But Fitz held up a hand. "Please repeat it back to me."

When he did with admirable accuracy, Fitz sent him back on his way with coin.

No movement from the house told Darcy he had some time before they would depart so he waved a servant over. "Please bring me a saddled horse. I have some business in town before we leave. And alert the others as to our delayed departure."

"Very good." The servant bowed and hurried off.

Even though Fitz grumbled to himself at being ordered about by his twin, he was rattled with news of more treachery from George Wickham. The man had almost destroyed their sister Georgiana. He had been a menace to the town of Derbyshire all growing up, and he had somehow cultivated their father's special attention.

He'd been given an appointment to the church which he gave up, instead favoring the military. But his hunger for more had obviously not been sated as gambling debts and unmet expenses followed him everywhere he went. But what he could hope for from a local woman of little means was a mystery. The families seemed respectable, though. He was hard pressed to imagine a scandal of any kind coming from Meryton. And yet, George seemed to bring about havoc in the best people's lives. Georgiana had truly thought him in love with her. Only when they'd shown proof of his visits to another woman on the very night they were to elope, did she give up her loyalty to the snake. But the immediate crumbling of her confidence right in front of their eyes had been heartbreaking for both brothers.

He clenched his fists. Oh, he'd find him all right. He'd find every last problem Wickham caused in that small town first. He'd expose him for what he was.

Sounds of another horse approached.

The servant walked up the main drive with his horse. Fitz waved him over. "Hurry, man. I must make haste."

The servant jumping to a run was gratifying to Fitz. And it helped alleviate his angst to begin. He was done waiting.

When at last the horse's reins were in his

hand, he leapt onto its back and was about to gallop swiftly in the direction of town when a voice carried to him. "Wait." A woman on a horse called out again. "Please. Wait."

He shifted his weight and turned his horse to see something he might remember forever.

Miss Jane sat astride a horse, her hair free and flowing out behind her in great golden waves. She rode at speeds he'd only seen men attempt and when she was almost upon him, pulled to a stop so quickly, he was afraid she might unseat herself. But she brushed the hair from her face and breathlessly asked, "Did I miss him?"

Fitz's heart thumped two extra times and he was filled with misgivings about their departure. Here was a woman who definitely cared.

"Um...no. You will find him up at the house, sort of despondently puttering about."

Her wavering mouth lifted at the corner. "I cannot allow him to leave without first speaking. I...cannot." Her eyes welled and he waved her on.

"Say no more. Please. Go find him at once."

She nodded and then took off again at breakneck speed down the front drive to Netherfield.

Fitz shook his head. He'd never been so wrong about a couple. He'd give a lot to see how that conversation changed things. But he had other work to do, and with any luck, he'd have some answers.

CHAPTER 12
JANE AND ELIZABETH

Jane had never done anything so reckless. But here she was, tearing up to the front drive on a horse, almost to the door of the Bingley estate. A servant appeared on the front stoop, and Caroline's face with open mouth stood out in an upper window. But Jane cared not for any of them. She had one wish only, and that was to see her beloved Charles.

Her horse skidded to a stop in response to her pulling back on the reins. She'd have to give that animal ample oats and grain for his assistance today.

Charles appeared on the front steps and then the rest of the world went away. All was quiet, all was diminished in sight, except for him. "Charles."

"Jane."

She sucked in a breath at the use of her first name. Up to that moment, he hadn't dared. But the sound of it on his lips rushed through her like a great storm and gave her the courage to say what she needed to say. "Oh, Charles, you mustn't go!"

He started as though truly shaken, and then a great light filled his face. Every line or concern disappeared behind his smile. He approached until he stood at her side, his face turned up to see her on the horse. Then when he spoke, his words were soft, intimate sounding. "Say the word and I'll stay. Or go. Or walk or run. I'm yours to command."

Jane could hardly speak for the joy that suddenly choked in her throat. But she must tell him all. He must know of Lydia and...Wickham and the scandal that would befall them. "Oh, Charles. You may wish to have nothing to do with me."

"Certainly not, ever my dearest." His eyes had so much kindness, so much trust. She almost quaked in fear and abandoned her purpose.

"I...I want always to be with you. But I'm afraid. There is much I must tell you. Something has happened."

He immediately reached for her. "Then let's get you off this animal so that I might converse with you properly." His hands gripped her waist, but it was no easy dismount when not riding side saddle; not when attempting to be appropriate.

Eventually, with some embarrassed laughs, he tugged at her backwards, hips first, both legs following.

With both feet on the ground at last, she leaned her back against him a moment. "Thank you. You do not know how much I felt as though I carried my life in my hands the whole ride here." And he would never know the extent of her inner angst and worry about how she could ever find happiness again. She still did not know, and she was as yet unsure she could place such a responsibility on Mr. Bingley. He was, after all, surely concerned for his own social well-being as well as that of his future children.

He turned her to face him. "Oh, my darling.

Your hands are shaking." He lifted them to his lips and kissed them both multiple times. "Tell me. What has happened?"

She stared into his face, almost quaking and giving up on her purpose. But his eyes were kind. His face trusting. He stood as close as was appropriate. And after but a few breaths, it all came tumbling out. "It's Lydia. It cannot be concealed. She has been absconded by George Wickham." The words rushed out as quickly as she could rid her lips of them. She held her breath, watching his face. Most men, nearly all men, would turn from her now and leave the area as he had planned, as he was packing trunks to do already.

Charles frowned, his eyes studying a piece of Jane's hair above her right shoulder. But after only a moment more, he nodded. "What has been done to rescue her?"

Jane's breath left her body in such a great wave of relief she almost collapsed against him again. "I don't exactly know. My father and my uncle who lives in London have been in conversation." She started to shake again. "Oh dear." Her teeth chattered. "I don't know what's the matter with me, but I'm suddenly so c-c-cold."

She leaned against him to steady herself, but the world started spinning and soon went very dark.

* * *

Elizabeth arrived home to complete mayhem. Her mother had taken to her bed, wailing and calling for her salts, keeping the servants and their sister Kitty rushing around to meet her every need. Her father was nowhere to be seen. She went in search of Jane, but to no avail. At length, she stopped their servant Mrs. Hill, who carried linens on one hip and a tea tray in the other hand. "Please, Mrs. Hill. Where is Jane?"

"Oh, bless her, my poor child. She left hours ago, yesterday even, on your father's horse. Word was, she was off to convince Mr. Bingley to stay here."

"What? Was she in her right mind?"

At that, Mrs. Bennet commenced calling, "Hill! Hill! Where are you, Hill?"

"Go. I'll find her."

Their loyal servant turned without another glance and rushed off to her mistress.

Elizabeth puzzled this turn. She'd gone after Mr. Bingley? On horseback? Jane was many things, but not a horsewoman. She found Mary, who looked as confused and concerned as she. "What has happened?" Mary's eyes were wide and concerned.

Kitty was not in her room. They went out the back entrance to a side garden. She was not there either. "Please tell me Kitty, too, has not disappeared."

"Where is Jane?"

"I'm going after her as soon as I figure that out."

They made their way to the barn and at last, in the back corner, they found Kitty. She had found a new litter of puppies and held one to her face, pacing the small space. She mumbled to herself, incomprehensible words, slightly panicked-sounding phrases. She was so lost in her own concerns, she didn't seem to notice the squirming puppy or their approach.

Lizzie and Mary exchanged a glance and then Lizzie said, "Kitty?"

Their youngest sister stopped but then she turned from them, bowing her head over the puppy.

They stepped nearer, Mary putting her arm across Kitty's shoulder.

"Come, Kitty, tell us what has happened?"

For a moment she said nothing but then her shoulders dropped, her head bowed further, and she whispered, "It's all my fault."

Lizzie hurried to her other side. "Come, Kitty, it cannot be all your fault. Lydia is perfectly capable of making her own choices, Jane too. And Mother, well, Mother is dealing with this the best she knows how."

But she shook her head and looked away.

The puppy squirmed so much she dropped to the ground. "Oh dear!" Kitty clutched at her dress. But the puppy landed on all four paws. "Wish that happened for people, too."

"What, dear?" Lizzie tried to tuck a piece of her unruly hair behind an ear.

"When they fall, they always land right." She sniffed. But then her lip quivered and she lowered her head in her hand.

"Come, Kitty. Talk to me." Lizzie turned her so that they faced one another. "What happened?"

"Oh, Lizzie! I wish you had been here! I didn't know. I didn't know." She cried into her hands. "Wickham is so handsome, so good to us all. He bought us ribbons. Everyone loves Wickham." She shook her head. "How could he have done this?"

"Tell me."

"He told her to meet him after an assembly dance back by the stables." She sniffed. "We all thought he was having a bit of fun. She talked about a kiss maybe." Kitty shrugged.

"Which would not have been advisable either." Mary frowned. "You know that, right?"

"Yes, Mary. We know." Kitty shook her head.

"Leave Mary be. She's just trying to help you. And she's correct. A woman going in the dark to meet a man to kiss him would be nearly as disastrous as leaving with him."

Kitty considered her a moment and then she nodded. "I see what you mean."

"People can declare a woman ruined for all manner of things, but mostly for being alone with a man in a compromising situation." Lizzie shook her head. "I feel it a bit ridiculous myself. But Mary is exactly right."

"I'm sorry. I know you're just trying to help."

"So, I'm assuming Lydia went to meet him?" Perhaps there would be some clue, some hint in the retelling that would help.

"At first, no. But then there was talk of other

women going to meet him. There were ladies hoping to be the one with him back behind the barn." Kitty shook her head. "And when Lydia heard that, she had to beat them all out. She almost ran out the back door."

Lizzie pressed her lips together but stayed silent.

"I followed her but as soon as she saw me, she shooed me away. She told me Wickham wouldn't do anything if she was not alone." Kitty shook her head. "That's when I should have known things weren't right."

"How could you have? We've never met anyone like this."

"So I stayed back. But I followed in the dark." She swallowed. "And I should have said something, done something."

"What happened?" Lizzie's hands went cold.

"She ran to him and they embraced. And then he kissed her." Kitty's mouth twisted in distaste.

"What's wrong?"

"It didn't look like a kiss should be."

"What do you mean?"

"Well, it was more...forced, harsh or something. I always thought it would be slow and sensitive and romantic." She closed her eyes. "Lydia must not have liked it either because she pushed away. But he pulled her back and would have kept kissing her. She twisted in his arms. He grabbed her. Then they said something, hushed whispers. She relaxed. She laughed. So I thought everything was fine. But then..." She hiccupped. "Then a carriage pulled around and they both climbed in!" She shuddered. "It all happened so fast." She wrapped her arms around her own middle. "I should have made a fuss when Lydia didn't like the kiss, right? That's when I should have done something?"

Mary pulled her close. "Kitty, I don't even know. At that point, she was ruined. So any fuss would have done her a lot of damage. She should not have been there in the first place. But that is not your choice or your fault."

Lizzie nodded. "Mary is correct. I wish she had not gone alone to see him. But here we are. Have you heard anything from her? Do you know their intentions?"

Kitty looked away.

"Kitty."

She pulled a crumpled piece of paper from her pocket. "She left me this."

"*Dear Kitty. You will think me the most romantic heroine when you hear what I've done. By the time you read this, I will be a married woman, the first of the Bennet sisters. Not even Jane will be first in this.*"

Lizzie shook her head. But Mary reading over her shoulder said, "It shows she had every intention of marrying. It shows that she hoped to do things the right way...sort of."

"Yes, except for the running away part, she hoped to marry." Lizzie nodded. "You're right."

"Then is everything going to be fine? Will they?" Kitty had so much hope Lizzie hated to dash it, but there was little to entice Wickham to marry Lydia. They'd both be abysmally poor for the whole of their lives.

"I don't know, Kitty. I can't imagine that was Mr. Wickham's intent, but I am happy to hear it was Lydia's."

Kitty folded the paper back up. "Are you going to tell Mama?"

"That you knew?" Lizzie considered her for a moment. "I think you should tell Papa. It might assist him in the search."

"Is there any hope? Will he find them?" Kitty

shook her head, answering her own question. "It would take a miracle."

"And we believe in those. We must not lose hope." Mary linked arms with her sister.

The three moved toward the house. Lizzie could hear her mother calling out even from where they stood in the back garden. "We must assist where we can. I will be going immediately after Jane." She stopped. "Kitty. What was Jane's intention?"

"I don't know. She just said she needed Bingley and asked for a horse to be saddled."

"This was yesterday."

"Yes, we received word that she'd caught a cold and would be spending the night."

"Oh! Oh, well, I must go to her right away."

Kitty nodded.

Mary stood taller. "We will assist with Mama and send any news from Father."

"Thank you." Elizabeth turned from them both, hurrying in the direction of Netherfield on foot. Jane had taken the only horse that was ridable.

CHAPTER 13
FITZWILLIAM

itz was more and more disgusted with Wickham the longer he followed his trail. His military commanding officer had little good to say of him. The local tenants and working class were not missing him, that much was certain. Several maids were suspiciously hidden from sight. He'd racked up an obscene amount of debt in a short amount of time. And everything Darcy learned told him that the man had no honorable intentions toward the Bennet girl. Fitz was left in a moral quandary. The more he exposed the man, the worse things would be for Lydia Bennet and therefore for her family. The best thing possible for her family would be for her to marry

Wickham quietly and for them to live far away. In that way, all reputations would be salvaged. Miss Lydia would undoubtedly have a terrible marriage, but if there was a way for Wickham to have a living, perhaps they could make good of this ill begone path.

He stood outside the largest of Wickham's debtors and closed his eyes. He would love to just expose the scoundrel and be done with him forever. If they'd done so initially, Wickham would not now be able to prey on innocence like he was.

But the same moral dilemma had faced them then. To preserve Georgiana's self-respect and her reputation, they swept the whole thing away.

He did not know Miss Lydia at all. He'd seen her rather overly emotional and loud self at two gatherings of the local gentry outside of Meryton, and he'd seen little he admired in her or in the family. The eldest two sisters aside, the Bennets had little to recommend them, admittedly. He knew the eldest two to be beyond reproach, and he had a surprising amount of thoughts directed at Miss Elizabeth. Even though he'd refused to ask her to dance, she had intrigued him. So be it. Here he was attempting to ease her situation. Beyond his admiration for her, he could not help or ease his sense of responsibility for the wrongs Wickham had committed, knowing Darcy could have prevented such a thing to occur, could have warned the whole area and the military of his character. Fitz did not often trouble himself in the affairs of others. But this situation with Wickham hit too close to home. He'd hidden his worry from his siblings, but Georgiana's almost fall had worried him more than anyone would guess.

Having Wickham handled by the military had been a relief to both he and his brother. They'd somehow mistakenly believed they could now wash their hands of him. Unfortunately, they were gravely mistaken, and now Miss Lydia and her family were suffering the consequences. His friend Charles might also be suffering the consequences by either associating with such a scandal through Miss Jane or distancing himself and therefore being deprived of his love. The idea that one man, one despicable human, could cause so much upheaval was inconceivable. And Darcy should have the means to put a stop to him. He should have done so long ago.

But be that as it may. Truth had a way of making itself known and freeing everyone of the bondage of deceit and secrets and lies. He had to trust such a thing for his current situation even though he'd been too fearful to trust before. Truth had a way of making things right.

He made a decision. He was going to expose Wickham. Perhaps these people would stand by the Bennets, vouch for Lydia's good character, somehow keep the news quiet? He had not seen behavior that magnanimously demonstrated in any of his interactions with the gentleman's class but there was always a first. And it was time. The man had been left free to cause ruination and defamation long enough. He would expose him, his debauchery, and ask for help in tracking him down with Miss Lydia in tow. In truth, Wickham had already exposed himself all over town and with his commanding officers.

Any help anyone could give Fitz would take him one step closer.

As is, he knew where to look next. Wickham had an accomplice in his efforts to deceive Georgiana. And that accomplice lived in London.

Fitz left word everywhere he could and then made arrangements to travel to London. He had one more stop, possibly two, before making the quick journey.

He didn't know how much—or if—to apprise Charles and so he avoided Netherfield. Some things were best handled alone. He'd have to consider the best course of action regarding Charles and the loss of his heart to Miss Jane. He wasn't even certain what to advise his own self and his odd relationship with the man. He ran a hand through his hair not caring one whit that it was now a flyaway mess all over his head.

Horse hooves sounded outside Darcy's window. An express rider flew down the street and stopped at Darcy's door below. A servant brought the note. They'd found Wickham! He handed some coin to the servant for the rider and ordered his carriage prepared and things packed immediately.

If he made haste, everything could be resolved before sundown tomorrow. He pressed his lips together. Or it would all be ruined. So much depended on the next several hours.

CHAPTER 14

ELIZABETH

Lizzie hurried up the steps of Netherfield Park with Mary in tow. "I cannot believe she is here with only servants and Charles to care for her." Mary sniffed. "Caroline has left. It's hardly appropriate and with Lydia running off we can only be too careful."

"Don't be too quick to pass judgment, Mary. I bet Charles was the most attentive of hosts."

She snorted.

With half a smile, Lizzie shook her head. "And the most appropriate. I do not believe Charles would dare do a thing to damage our Jane no matter how much he'd want to."

"But the appearances."

Lizzie placed a hand on her sister's arm.

"Which is why we are here and why you are to remain."

"Is there a reason you are not the sister to stay? I would think you be the most suited. And the one Jane prefers."

Lizzie studied her sister but the expression that stared back was purposefully devoid of emotion. "Mary. She does not most prefer me. I do believe we are the closest friends. Closest in age you know. But she loves you all dearly. I hope you know that."

Mary hesitated a moment but then nodded. "I do. She is the kindest and most caring. I lack for nothing as her sister."

Lizzie vowed to do better by way of Mary. She was definitely a much-overlooked member of the family.

"It needs to be you because someone has to manage our mother."

Mary did not respond, but Lizzie guessed she'd far rather care for Jane than for Mother's fits and blaming the world for her daughter's plight. Lizzie wanted to be there to hear any news of Lydia as well. Perhaps there was some reason to hope, some small chance that all would still be saved.

Darcy's laughing, teasing eyes came to her mind. Her heart sped. He was so much more than she'd ever given him credit for being. He was kind and giving and caring. She could not account for his behavior toward them in Meryton, but at the house party and since, he'd been all that she'd ever want in a man's treatment. She sighed. And so very handsome. Her cheeks colored. Why had he stepped in where Jane and Bingley were concerned? Perhaps all was well now that she was apparently at Netherfield?

"Are you well, Lizzie?" Mary studied her closely.

Lizzie fanned herself. "I do hope so." She shook her head. "I am not ill, that is for certain. Now come. Let's at least alert the servants we are lurking on their doorstep."

But as they approached the front door, it opened and Charles appeared on the foot tails of their butler.

The servant stepped aside, bowing.

"Please come in. Miss Bennet, Miss Bennet. I am too pleased to see you. I do believe Jane will be much relieved." He bowed over their hands and then led them up the stairs. "I have asked the servants to give you whatever you require.

Please ask for refreshment for both yourselves and for Jane. I confess I am at a loss and she is... unwell. It concerns me greatly to see her unwell." His face was filled with so much concern that Lizzie stopped in the hall and placed a hand on his arm. "Please do not concern yourself. She is strong and will recover, I am certain. Your care here cannot be lacking in any way." She gave him an extra squeeze and then hurried toward the door he indicated.

The room was lovely but dark and a bit musty. Against the far wall, with covers to her chin, Jane lay shivering.

"Oh, my dear Jane." She rushed to her side. "Mary, open the drapes please, and the windows."

"Lizzie, you've come." The hand she reached to grasp Lizzie's was weak and clammy. Her head felt hot to the touch and damp with sweat. Lizzie pulled back her covers.

Jane groaned. "No, I am freezing."

"But you're burning up. We have to get your fever to drop." She turned to a waiting maid. "Please bring me a bowl of water and cloths to lay on her head. Also, your cook's best remedies for fever and a broth for her to drink."

The maid bobbed a curtsey and hurried from the room.

A soft knock and the reopening of the door a crack made Lizzie smile. Bingley's head poked in. "Is there anything you lack? Any other way I can possibly be of assistance?"

Jane pulled a pillow over her face. "Oh, Charles. You cannot see me thus."

"You are beautiful no matter how I see you, Jane. Be well. Please be well."

"She will be. I've sent the maid for things. Thank you for your kindness. We shall get her right as can be hopefully very soon."

He nodded, looking past Lizzie to get a glimpse of Jane.

"Can he come in to see you?" Lizzie whispered.

But after a moment, the pillow moved as if Jane nodded.

"I do believe you may come to visit her." Lizzie stood. "Mary will be with you. And I shall get ourselves situated for a moment while we wait for the servants to bring the required items."

He rushed to Jane's side and scooped up her hands in his. "Oh, my dear Jane. Jane darling. I cannot believe you are thus. We will do all in our power until you are as well as you have ever been. All that I have is at your disposal. If there is anything at all I can do to bring greater happiness and wellness."

Jane lifted her fingers to his mouth. "Hush, my Charles. You are all that is good. If I might rest here, I do believe I shall be as well as ever." She smiled, her lips dry and her eyes watery and clouded with fever.

But Bingley looked on as though she were the loveliest angelic human he'd ever seen. And in truth, she likely was. Jane was special indeed.

Lizzie nodded to Mary who would be the most diligent of chaperones, certainly, and then stepped across the hall. The view from that room covered the entire valley in that direction. It was a lovely situation and from the looks of things, would be all in Jane's care not too soon a day. As long as wide-spread knowledge of a scandal could be avoided.

She sighed.

Prevention of the gossip spreading was all but impossible. She could not imagine the whole world not knowing.

But who knew now? No one yet. Except for

Mr. Darcy and her family. She kneaded her hands together.

She left Jane in Mary's care in a much-improved state. Her fever was lower. And she was in good spirits.

But she arrived home to a front room full of Lucases with way too many questions.

Lizzie greeted them all. "I'm sorry, my mother is indisposed. Let me order tea for you." She waved to Hill who immediately left to take care of things and to hopefully keep their mother's wails to a minimum.

"How is your mother?" Mrs. Lucas was a dear woman but the gleam in her eye told Lizzie she had also come for any bit of news and to confirm her suspicions.

"She is quite unwell to be honest. Something has really bothered her constitution. She is quite consumptive even and carries on about her nerves." Lizzie shook her head. "She might be quite contagious and so she is keeping to her rooms with no visitors at the moment."

Mrs. Lucas sat back in her chair a moment as though Lizzie herself were carrying the very thing plaguing their mother. Which of course she was, in a less obvious manner. Lizzie carried her worries and concerns hidden beneath the surface where her mother wore them like a medal.

The tea arrived and everyone spoke of the assembly at Meryton and the many dances they'd all enjoyed.

"And what of Lydia? Kitty?" Mrs. Lucas waved a fan in her face in an odd attempt to stave off the boredom.

"They are out." Lizzie shrugged. "I do apologize. I am a weak substitute for the rest of the Bennets. But perhaps you'd like to see Mary's needlepoint?" She stood as though to fetch it, but a slight groan and obvious dislike of the idea brought Mrs. Lucas to her feet. "Well, do tell your mother we were here to see to her well-being. She is as dear to me as any woman. There are nasty rumors about town and I wish to stave them off. Wickham has left too abruptly, left his post, and was perhaps seen with a young woman. No one can as yet identify his victim or if she be willing or no." Mrs. Lucas clucked, eyeing Lizzie's face too closely.

But though her heart nearly stopped and her hands ran cold, she shook her head as casually as she could. "What terrible news. I thought him the most congenial, the best manners. I think him incapable..." She tapped her fingers on her legs. "Perhaps no woman was involved at all, merely Wickham running? Has he anything to run from?" Her eyes widened in the pretended innocence of being unaware. But her nails dug into her palm in the hand she clenched together under her skirts.

"I did hear he had much debt in town, people coming after for repayment." She nodded wisely. "Perhaps you are right and none of our young ladies has been foolish enough to fall for his entrapments." Her eyes narrowed. "I thought you were once enamored with the man."

Lizzie gasped. "Goodness no. He was pleasing to look at to be sure, but no part of me was considering him as anything other than a distraction, I assure you."

She nodded, appearing satisfied. "And your sisters. Nothing in them would attract a man such as he. You have nothing to offer." She stood. "No, there is nothing for it. He must have preyed upon a servant or tenant family, or no woman is involved. I shall stop the idle talk at once."

"Have you called upon all the others, then?"

She shrugged. "One has to know how to act and who to protect, doesn't one?"

Lizzie tipped her head to the side. "Yes, one does. I'd be so sick if he ruined the life and reputation of one of our own."

"We won't allow that to happen. We women must band together in situations such as these." Her eyes burned with an intensity Lizzie was not suspecting, but she loved her for it. Even though she could not reveal why, she hugged her fiercely. "Thank you for that. Let us pray no one is involved."

"Yes, let's. Do give Lydia and Kitty my regards."

"I will. I know my Aunt and Uncle Gardiner will be here shortly to take us all up on holiday to the Lake Country, but I'm certain they shall be by either before or after to discuss the events."

"Yes, I'm certain as well." She moved to the door. "Come, ladies."

The Lucases hustled to the door just as the mail arrived.

Mrs. Lucas's keen gaze caused Lizzie to gather it without glancing down at the tray and she curtseyed her farewells once again while the servants shut the door after their guests.

She fell against the wall. "Whew. That was something."

But good had come from the interview. No one knew for certain what Wickham had done. Lydia's name was as yet, safe. And Mrs. Lucas seemed a powerful ally.

Kitty peeked her head around the corner of the stairs. "Have they gone?"

"Oh, Kitty!" Lizzie smiled. "It was smart of you to stay hidden."

She nodded. "I thought perhaps it would make more sense for Lydia to be gone from the house if I were absent as well."

"You are too correct." Lizzie hugged her sister. "Jane is as well as can be expected. We wait to hear her fever has truly dropped, but I don't think she is in any danger."

"Oh good." Kitty looked to the mail in Lizzie's hands. "Do we have any news?"

Lizzie lifted the pile, and they sifted through it quickly but saw no news from their father or uncle or anyone else.

CHAPTER 15
ELIZABETH

The next morning, Lizzie was awakened by shouts from downstairs. She wrapped a robe about herself and hurried toward the sound. The shouts sounded more like hysterics, and she rounded the corner to see Kitty producing the surprisingly loud agitations. But Lizzie forgot all about her sister's noise when she saw the cause.

Lydia.

Her hair was mussed, parts standing in knotted messes and parts flattened to the side of her head. The dark circles under her eyes made her expression seem even more hollow, but her eyes were dark, her face drawn, and no sound came from her mouth. In truth, she hardly looked at any of them.

Lizzie approached. "Lydia?" Her voice was quiet, gentle, but Lydia jumped.

"Hm?"

"Welcome home, sister." Lizzie pulled her into an embrace. For a moment, she was stiff and then she relaxed into Lizzie. Her breath came out as a sigh and she rested her face into Lizzie's shoulder. "It is good to be home."

Lizzie held her a moment more and then their mother's shrieks and shouts from upstairs interrupted them all. "Lydia!! Oh, my baby is home! Come here this minute. Have you brought us a handsome husband?"

Lizzie winced.

Their father stepped across the threshold. He looked tired and worn. The glance he spared Lizzie was brief but grim.

Lydia turned from them and stepped slowly up the stairs.

Kitty followed, her expression uncertain.

When at last they were alone, Lizzie turned to her father. "What has happened?"

He pinched the bridge of his nose. "Enough for me to sit in solitude for weeks on end. I fear I deserve it. Though, I deserve to be endlessly tormented. To think she is returned with so little bother or trouble to any of us; I cannot fathom how it was accomplished."

"And her well-being? Is she...well?" She wished to ask if she'd been truly compromised, if she had been hurt?

But her father shook his head. "Only she knows the answer to that question. Wickham promises that he did nothing to her."

Lizzie breathed out her relief and nearly fell against the wall. "Can it be so?"

"It appears to be."

"Then perhaps, just for a moment, we might feel hope that the information is contained. The Lucases were here, and the missus is determined to defend Lydia's name and all others. The story is that Wickham left alone."

Her father nodded. "Then there truly is hope for us all, isn't there?" He looked so forlorn, so without hope that she rushed to his side. "Father?"

"I am merely unhappy with my own behavior. I will indeed be more careful with you all."

Lizzie could only nod, for she agreed that stronger care needed to be taken and she would be happy for her father to take a greater interest in all their lives.

A servant arrived with the post on a platter.

Her father lifted a small stack. "This is more than I expected." He filed through the envelopes and stopped on one, his eyebrow raised. "To what do we owe the pleasure of a correspondence with Mr. Collins? Is your dear Charlotte Lucas well?"

"I believe so. They've been married but a few short months, but she's already sequestered a room for her own particular use. They dine at Rosings Park regularly and she seems almost as enamored with their patron, the esteemed Lady Catherine De Bourgh, as is her husband." Lizzie shrugged, thinking briefly of the man's odious marriage proposal to her before he left to ask her best friend. "I'd never be happy there, but she seems to be so."

"No Lizzie, you need a man you can respect, love even, who challenges you, excites your mind."

Her father kept talking about men who read and intelligent conversation, all things Lizzie had heard before and greatly valued, but all she could think about in that moment was Mr. Darcy. He'd proven to be everything her father was describing. But the different accounts of him were quite puzzling to her. His comment about her being handsome enough, his inability to even remember her or her family from his visit to Netherfield, so many things, his interference with Jane and then with Mary... He was not at all what he seemed. She knew that to be true. But when she stood near him, when he looked into her eyes, she could only see sincerity and true caring. She didn't know what to make of him.

And now, she regretted deeply telling him of Lydia's scandal. Now that it might well be soon forgotten, he knew. And no matter what she thought of him, he would surely wish to have nothing more to do with her or the family. She sighed. Thoughts of Mr. Darcy reminded her that someone should be notifying Jane and Mary of the good news. She summoned a servant and wrote a quick missive to her sisters. "Please deliver this at once." She added a suggestion that she tell Charles immediately of the good news so that perhaps he might feel even more free to associate once again with their family.

Though, from the looks of things, he had never deserted them.

Her father had opened up the letter from Mr. Collins and read it with a frown. "There is a portion of this for you from Charlotte." He took out a folded bit and handed it to her but she glanced over the page from Mr. Collins first to see what caused her father's furrowed brow.

Mr. Collins waxed eloquently about all things Rosings Park. He discussed at length Charlotte's good fortune in marrying him, describing their situation in great detail. Then he closed with the statement, *"We were saddened to hear of the recent escapades of cousin Lydia. With any luck she is returned safely though we are saddened that things for her and your family by association can never be the same. We are distantly at your service. Charlotte still wishes to receive you and because the details are vague at best, Lady Catherine has given her approval but she will want a full accounting when you are here so that she might determine our best future course of action. As you well know, one cannot be too careful with one's associations."*

Lizzie clenched her fists. "Of all the pompous..."

Her father held up his hand. "Look at the post script."

She squinted. Yes, he'd written a few more faded lines. "*We have just received news from Charlotte's family that indeed Lydia was not involved with the recent Mr. Wickham's tarnish. What a relief that must be for all of you. We are certainly relieved and renew the warmth of our invitation to come at your earliest convenience. No mention needs to be made of the aforementioned stain.*"

"Oh he's so loathsome. I don't know how Charlotte abides his presence."

"Yes, it sounds like she is making the most of her experience and has time to herself. Managing a home and caring for her own life might be all she hoped for. We mustn't challenge people's right to joy in their own choices because they are different from ours." Her father patted her shoulder. "I am much relieved and grateful to the Lucases for their swift response and squelching of rumors. However true the rumors may have been." He wiped his brow. "We are greatly in their debt."

"Mr. Bennet!!" Lizzie's mother's shouts could be heard all throughout their gardens.

Her father lifted the corner of his mouth. "It is good to be the deliverer of good news, is it not?"

She smiled. "It most certainly is."

He stepped slowly toward the stairs. Never did he shout in response to her mother's shrieks. But he plodded along to find her in the house to see what it was that she desired.

Lizzie lowered to a small sofa to read Charlotte's letter, curious about how they had come to know of Wickham's disappearance in the first place.

Charlotte began immediately with the problem at hand. *"Oh Lizzie. The most dreadful news reached us. I have done my best to cast doubt, and Mother's latest express that Father sent squelched the wagging tongues, but there is still a good amount of suspicion. I'm including Lydia, Kitty, and Mary in my invitation to come to call. I think it will do them good and will show without doubt that Lydia is indeed still with her family and well and untainted."*

Lizzie cringed.

Charlotte added, *"I hate to use such a word, but I speak as though I'm reacting as Lady Catherine might. She is not one to tolerate much of anything, particularly something that challenges her sense of correctness."*

Lizzie snorted. "I would not enjoy living near such a woman." Frustration with Mr. Collins and Lady Catherine would always be there, but she could only feel a blanket of warmth and gratitude for her friend Charlotte. She sat at a writing desk to draft a response immediately.

She accepted the invitation for her sisters and herself. She thanked her for protecting their good names and reputations and assured her that Lydia was indeed home and safe and sound with them, but that Wickham had built quite an awful reputation for himself with debts and scandal all around him. *"Can you believe I once thought him entertaining? I quake at the thought."* She'd vilified Mr. Darcy for slighting her and celebrated Wickham because he spoke pretty things to her and pet her vanity. Of the two, Mr. Darcy, though awkward and ill spoken, and meddling, was likely a better man. But interfering with Jane? She could not account for it. There was nothing there but goodness. Once again she was at a loss to understand the man. She tried to shift him from her mind.

As she returned to her letter, she caught

Charlotte up on news from town and on her life, detailing much about the house party but leaving out her interactions with Mr. Darcy. She was at a loss to explain him, and Charlotte had experienced the bulk of her strong dislike and prejudice against the man. She didn't have anything to add by way of explanation for her feelings. She didn't even know her own feelings. She held her head in her hands as though trying to understand what went on inside of it. How could she like a man who was not likable in so many ways? With no answers, she tried to make sense of it all to no avail. And then, giving up, she finished her letter and went to go find Lydia.

CHAPTER 16
JANE

J ane sat in a small and lovely sitting room just off her bedroom at Netherfield Park. She had a book in her lap but she was staring out across the vast expanse of land surrounding the estate. Charles entered. By the fall of his feet, she knew it was him without turning to look into his face. She smiled. "You are too good to me you know."

"Not nearly good enough. I'm just relieved to see you improving enough to be here, sitting up, in the sitting room." He smiled, seeming to know he was not wording things in half as eloquent a manner as could be done, but not caring. "This is one of my favorite rooms, you know."

She turned to him then, taking in the joy in

his face, his constant smiles, his perpetual good nature that always seemed to shine from him— she didn't know how she'd become so lucky, so blessed as to deserve him. Nothing had been said yet, of course. But his feelings, his intentions, seemed clear.

One thing troubled her. Why had he been so willing to leave, to desert her?

She pulled out her recent missive from Lizzie. "Good news. Lydia has returned and was spared any true harm. No one seems to know of her leaving with Wickham and perhaps, social damage has been kept to a minimum." Tears filled her eyes. And with shaking hands she reached one arm to him. "I'm so relieved."

He immediately came to her side, holding her hand to his chest. "I would have stood by you through it all, weathered whatever scandal." His eyes were wide and earnest. She didn't say it, but she knew it would have been a challenge indeed, perhaps better they left Society if that had been the case. Their children would have struggled. Nothing easy would have come of such a union but she had loved him, she did love him, so much she could not lose such a man, money or no, status or no. She wanted to be with

Charles. "Thank you. I..." She wiped her tears anew. "I don't deserve you." She laughed. "There is not much more to say than that. You are too good. Too kind. Too much. It's no wonder I love you so." She gasped. And then held a hand to her mouth, her face heating. She'd never admitted as much to him before. And she didn't know what to do now that she'd said the words that hummed through her with every thought. She dared a look into his eyes.

He was shining even more so if such a thing were possible. The earnestness in his gaze, the intensity of his expression stole her breath. He lifted her fingers and kissed each one, intently earnest, his lips pressing on them, their knuckles or their tips, the attention sending shivers up her arms. "I, my dear Jane, most ardently and dare I say, passionately, love you too." She daren't look away, she daren't move or even breathe. He knelt beside her chair so that their faces were closer together. His head tilted just enough that he could kiss her if he so desired. She pressed her teeth into her bottom lip, sure and unsure at the same time. He moved closer and stared into her eyes, sent silent promises to her, promises she understood but could never give word to. Then he nodded and created some space between them. "Oh, my dear Jane. I wish you well of course, but I don't want to lose your presence here in my home. In truth, I'd like to never lose it."

"Then you shall have it." She waved her fingers in the air. "But I do hope I shall be well enough to enjoy it. There seem to be many vistas and places to see and walk and enjoy out this window."

"Oh there are, and we shall explore each and every one." His grin grew, and Jane almost laughed at his exuberance.

She could sit and listen to his promises, his proclamations of love, his assurances all day. But something had made him wish to desert her once, something had turned him from this loving, doting man to one so dismissive as to depart with naught but a note from his sister. Something in him fell short of the constant beacon she dared to trust with her heart.

She didn't mention whatever that something might be, not yet; but they would talk of it. She would watch and hope that it disappeared, whatever this inconstancy, this crack in his reliability seemed to be. She would not risk her whole heart and livelihood on someone who could withdraw his affections at any time, whose affections were of the weak and faltering sort, swayed by others or passing whims. He certainly fell in love quickly, but could he stay? That was the full question, and Jane had seen enough of her parents' bickering and her father's seeming loss of love and respect for her mother for Jane to question the lasting nature of any man's declarations but especially Bingley who she stood to lose so much of her heart to, who had already once threatened to break it.

But she had time for such discoveries. Thanks to Lydia's return, she had a chance to even consider such a luxury as a marriage for love. She smiled and turned the fullness of her happiness and relief to Charles. "I am so blessedly happy right now."

He pulled up a chair next to her and held her hand against his chest. "I hope that every day can be full of moments where I hear you say those words over and over again." His heart pounded underneath her hand that he clutched close.

"Just the thought of you brings about such

joy, my Charles." She dipped her head, shy about her transparency.

But he lifted her chin with his finger and stared into her eyes a moment before leaning back in his chair to stare out at the remarkable view once again. Her hand still pressed against his heart. It still hammered. And she didn't think much would change for many hours hence, for which she was perfectly content.

CHAPTER 17
ARTHUR DARCY

rthur Darcy's carriage was nearly home in Derbyshire when he was met with a rider, carrying a note from his brother. He read the news of Wickham's debts and things in town with great interest. And then he was even more pleased to see his brother exerting himself in every possible way to bring justice to the man who had caused so much pain, had hurt so many. Fitz was on a crusade of sorts and would not stop until the man was deported. Which was fine with Arthur. Their father, even as deceived as he'd been by Wickham, at this point in their evidence against him would have gladly had him shipped abroad.

Arthur pitied the Australians. No one deserved such a man. He could be quite charming. That was the problem, rewarding good behavior with marked attention, physical rewards, compliments, and time. All of which was withdrawn as soon as one did not meet expectations or no longer proved to be of use. A person could get quite addicted to Wickham and his charm, working harder and harder for the praise, the love, the attention. But no longer. Not in England, at any rate. Arthur was proud of Fitz. Perhaps the man was at last growing up and taking responsibility for his actions, his life, and with any luck, his estate.

Then he approached the end of the letter where Fitz wrote, *"I don't think I will be making my way to Rosings at any rate. I'll send my regrets to our aunt. I feel an urgency to return to Pemberley. Suddenly, brother, I feel as though I should meet at least some of the expectations you all have of me. And from there, I can do more to ensure Wickham's swift departure."*

Arthur could only be pleased with this news. But it created a large inconvenience for himself. Because as was typical of his brother, he did not consider that if Fitz didn't go to Rosings, Arthur would have to. There were papers that needed to be signed And meetings with their aunt's steward. There was a chance he and Fitz could stand to inherit the whole of it, but that depended completely upon a distant cousin producing an heir. And Darcy did not want to think about other people's lives in such a way. He was content with what he had been given to manage. If Rosings fell to him and his brother, he would naturally work to maintain it as well, but it would increase his responsibilities tenfold.

Whatever happened in the future, he and his brother were some of the few remaining male relatives in Lady Catherine's life, and although she didn't seem to need any protection, he felt bound to answer her summons and provide assistance where he or his brother could. So since Fitz was returning home to Pemberley, Arthur would need to make his way to Rosings.

Suddenly he was tired. The promise of his soft bed and excellent chef were calling to him. He would hurry home for a moment, refresh his belongings, and then be off to Rosings in the next few days. But oh, how he longed to linger in his home.

He rapped on the ceiling and the carriage

began to move again. Just for a few days he would rest. Just a few.

CHAPTER 18
ELIZABETH

Their journey to meet their aunt and uncle in Derbyshire was a welcome diversion; even though it sat not in the least on the way to Rosings or to visit Charlotte, she could not begrudge her aunt a stop at her childhood home.

Lizzie sat close to Lydia in the carriage, at times reaching for her hand or patting her reassuringly on the knee with only a half-smile or brief acknowledgement in return. Her sister was not yet well, in fact in many ways, she seemed scared. Everything else about her was functioning. She ate. She slept. She conversed, but it was without the typical Lydia energy and with a certain hesitation in her eyes that had never been present before.

Lizzie should be thanking the stars for that hesitation because it would mean far fewer moments of family embarrassment at her sister's doing. But she could not find relief in something that seemed to diminish her sister's joy.

After an hour or so, Lydia lowered her head to Lizzie's shoulder and snuggled in closer. Lizzie's heart warmed further and a protectiveness filled her heart. Lydia behaved the way she did because she was young and no one was showing her a better manner in which to present herself. She'd been allowed to be out at far too early an age before the benefit of observing her sisters or even receiving any instruction at all. She tilted her head to rest her cheek on the top of Lydia's head.

Then her sister's voice, low and close to her ear, began telling the story of what happened.

"He wanted to meet to tell me a secret." She sighed. "That's what he said. A grand gossipy secret that I should be pleased to know before anyone else."

Lizzie grabbed her hand and gave it a

squeeze. Everyone else in the carriage was sleeping or not paying attention. She hoped Lydia would keep talking. She needed to and Lizzie wished to know how to help her sister.

"So I agreed to meet. It was all a grand adventure, I thought. He was paying me attention. I was singled out of all the women who thought him handsome." She reached up to wipe a tear with her other hand. "I ran to the barn, sure I'd beaten out all the other ladies." She shook her head. "But he embraced me and then kissed me so suddenly. I was shocked and pleased and then it was too much. It felt more like... I don't know what it felt like but not what I thought a kiss should be." She fell silent and Lizzie just waited. So much sorrow flowed through her at the thought of all Lydia had lost.

"I pulled away because I didn't like it. Then he stopped and said he was sorry. That I was just too beautiful in the moonlight. He wanted to show me something special... Things like that. So I..." She hiccupped and then her shoulders shook. "So I went with him. And there was never a chance to leave or anywhere else to go but with him. And I admit it was all so romantic. He held my hand. He spoke of sweet things we would do.

He promised to read me books and feed me chocolate tarts. He promised to sleep away our days and dance into our nights. But then he spoke of other things. Things I do not wish to know. You would be highly surprised what enters a man's mind Lizzie, and I tell you it is not what you would expect at all."

Lizzie kept her mouth from twitching, but only just. She nodded with the seriousness of the moment.

"He spoke of other things we would do, and that is when I knew I would have to leave him. What woman would agree to such things? What woman would ever allow a man such liberties? Surely our parents have never participated in such nonsense. Surely no woman truly has..." She searched Lizzie's face as though to confirm. Lizzie could only shrug. "You can be assured I have done nothing with any man."

She nodded again as though it was better that way. "But I could not be free of him. I didn't dare at first. Where would I go? Not until Brighton when I ran away to the militia commander did I ever feel free of him. He had to show up for duty you see. He left me alone in the apartment, and I made my escape, my hair a mess, my dress disheveled. I was quite a sight, but Mr. Darcy helped me, you know."

"Mr. Darcy!" She spoke too loudly and caught Mary's eye, but no one else was paying attention. She whispered, "What was he doing there?"

"I don't know. But he helped me find Mrs. Forster and the colonel and got me settled, and then he spoke to the colonel, and I think they talked to Wickham. I don't know or care. He never...we didn't..." She stopped. "I want you to know that in his own way he did respect me. He never again kissed me or the like." Her face turned brighter red. "I hope to never be approached with such an opportunity again."

Lizzie nodded, hoping Lydia remained firm in her determination for five more years at least. But she barely held back her anger with Wickham. There was no respect in convincing a young girl to run off with you, knowing you were likely ruining her and her family's lives and reputation forever. But she held her tongue in that regard. She could only be grateful. "Why do you suppose he did not pursue you further?"

Lydia shrugged. "I think in his own way, he really did care for me."

Lizzie supposed that could be true. But again, truly caring for a woman did not involve ruining her life. "Perhaps he hoped to gain something with which to live as well, for the both of you?"

Lydia shrugged again. "I don't care, about him or any man anymore." She sat up and looked Lizzie in the face, her eyes wide and sincere. "But Mr. Darcy is a good man, Lizzie." She dipped her head again and snuggled in closer. Soon her breathing became regular and Lizzie was sure she had fallen asleep. She lifted her head off of Lydia's and tried to process all that she had just heard. Lydia was safe. She'd been very brave; foolish, but brave. And Mr. Darcy had been there to help? How had such a thing come to be?

Her heart was pounding so hard in her chest she thought for sure Lydia would notice or Mary who sat at her left. Mary's eyes were open and she nodded toward Lydia and mouthed. "I heard."

Lizzie nodded.

Mary tilted her head. "Mr. Darcy?" She placed a hand at her heart.

Lizzie smiled and shrugged with one shoulder.

Then Mary closed her eyes, a small smile tugging at her lips.

Lizzie hoped for something wonderful for this amazing sister of theirs. Mary was a gem of a woman. She hoped for the best for all of them. When the chance for happiness had again resurfaced for the Bennet sisters after a possibility of it being lost forever, Lizzie clung to the notion. And she vowed to be a better help to her sisters.

But what to think of Mr. Darcy's involvement! She had no thoughts other than a wild hope that perhaps he had assisted for her benefit? Perhaps he truly cared. But as soon as the thoughts might have taken a precarious grip on her heart and hopes, she nudged them aside. He was perhaps in the right place at the right time or felt responsible to out the man or perhaps he had not assisted in quite the way Lydia remembered. She sighed. Her mind would ponder all possible scenarios for much of the night she was certain, and she would likely never have a chance to ask him or even to thank him. The mystery would remain unsolved. Dangling mysteries and the thought of never seeing him again battled it out as the worst outcome of the situation. To have something unanswered, unexplained, was a devastating occurrence for the curious of mind and most especially when the person involved had such a riveting capture of her attention.

CHAPTER 19
ELIZABETH

Weary and travelworn, the group arrived at the Inn in Derbyshire jointly with their Aunt and Uncle Gardener. Lizzie leapt from the carriage to embrace her aunt. "Oh, how good it is to see you!" She squeezed her tightly and received a kiss on her cheek.

"Lizzie my dear. You have been through so much. I hope you are well?" She stared into her eyes as though searching her soul.

"I am, Aunt. And Lydia is also. She is as well as can be. Mary and Kitty have joined us, but Jane sends her regrets."

Her aunt's smile grew. "Your mother has been keeping me abreast of the updates there.

Though I can hardly account for her grand effusions at times. She acts as though a wedding will happen tomorrow one minute and not for many months the next." She fanned her face.

"They are very much in love and quite pleased with themselves. That is all anyone knows at the moment, even Jane." Lizzie grinned. "And I have not seen a more deserving human for this kind of happiness. She is all smiles."

"Pleased I am to hear it." Aunt turned to the others, hugging and kissing them in turn. "And now we must freshen up, for I have a grand treat for you this very afternoon."

"What is it, Aunt?" Kitty walked with the skip of the young still. She twirled once for good measure then turned inquisitive eyes back on their aunt.

"How would you like to take a guided tour of Pemberley? It is the grandest home in the area, and has the finest library as well as sculpture garden of any I have seen."

Lizzie's heart clenched and she began to shake her head.

"Are the family in residence?" Mary placed a

hand on her forearm and she sent a grateful glance in her direction.

"No. They only open the house when no one is home."

Lizzie nodded, relief filling her. "Then we must. Let us see this grand house, shall we?"

They were all freshened up and ready to ride in the Inn's open chaise and four within the hour.

"The countryside is the loveliest I've seen." Lizzie breathed in the soft smells of earth and a hint of something green. "I'd give a lot to walk these meadows."

"And you shall. Why not?" Her aunt laughed. "We can employ the Inn's servants, if you like."

"I'd very much like."

"And I shall go with you." Mary surprised her with a new interest in walking.

She nodded. "Thank you. I welcome the company. But be aware. Once I begin, I find it difficult to stop. There is always something else to discover, isn't there?"

Mary laughed. "Especially in a new place." She shrugged. "I imagine it will be good for me. I'll try not to disrupt your plans with complaints or wishes to rest."

"Very good, Mary." Aunt Gardener smiled with a great warmth. "I look around at you all, and I feel so overwhelmed with happiness. You ladies are some of the finest I know. How good it is to be your aunt." She patted their knees in turn as they faced each other in the carriage.

Soon all talking ceased as they entered the lane to the great Pemberley estate. Lizzie was certainly speechless, and the others as well, it seemed. Every vista was lovely. Every turn brought new glorious things for the eye to feast upon. The grounds were cared for, it was obvious, and in a way that allowed plants to be wild and free. Not much trimming or containing of glorious flowers and rolling shrubbery. Winding stone walls made their way across large expanses of grass. As they turned another bend, a great pond came into view and in its reflection, Lizzie saw Pemberley for the first time.

A figure with a familiar gait walked toward the stables to the right of the house and for a moment, Lizzie was certain she'd seen Mr. Darcy, but then she shook her head. It could not be. The family was not in residence. But even still, the thought of seeing him like that, after knowing how he'd aided her sister, after thinking she'd never see him again, caused such a pounding in her heart she could scarcely catch her breath.

"Are you well, Lizzie?" Her Aunt Gardener reached a hand over to touch her forehead and the sides of her face.

"I—perhaps I just need a moment. I'm a bit lightheaded."

"Don't tell me Lizzie will take to the vapors like Mama!" Kitty fanned herself and pretended to fall back in a dramatic faint.

"No, Kitty. I shall not be fainting." She looked away as though to enjoy more of the vista, but her eyes scanned the area near the stables to prove she'd imagined things. She saw no one further. No matter. They would tour the home and then be gone from the place before any sight of Mr. Darcy.

With deep breaths, she counted slowly until they arrived at front of the door. Every place has a feel about it and this could be nothing but elegance. Understated, comfortable elegance. The front stairs were grand and beautiful stone. She was awed by it all. Mr. Darcy was the master of all this? She swallowed and then stepped up to the front door.

The butler had kindly eyes. "Whom shall I say is calling?"

Aunt Gardener smiled. "Good afternoon. We are the Bennet sisters and Mrs. Gardener and hoping for a tour of the lovely estate? I used to live in Derbyshire and have such fond memories."

A woman about the same age as Aunt Gardener approached with similar kindly eyes to that of the butler. "Welcome. You have come at the perfect moment for a tour. I have some time this morning dedicated to just such a pursuit before some responsibilities later."

"Thank you." Mrs. Gardener stood at her side and the two began chattering away about Derbyshire and some of the local families.

Lizzie smiled and took in her surroundings. The home was lovely and obviously very fine but not extravagant, not overstated, not wasteful. Things seemed comfortable, useful and organized. She smiled. There was such a strong aura of Mr. Darcy himself she could almost smell his soap.

They went through room after room, each exactly as she thought they should be, each comfortable and cheery and, well, perfect, so much so that Lizzie almost couldn't stand to be in such a place that would be forever outside her reach.

Dwelling on just such a thought, she stepped into the music room as the man himself stood up in front of them.

The housekeeper shook her head. "Oh, Mr. Darcy. Forgive us. I was not informed of your arrival."

"No matter. I first went to the stables. It's no problem at all." His eyes traveled over the group and stopped on her.

She sucked in a breath and then dipped a curtsey. "Mr. Darcy."

"Ah yes, Miss...Elizabeth, was it?" He dipped a quick bow, but showed no further sign of recognition. "Please feel at home. In fact, I'm certain Cook can provide tea for our guests?" He nodded to his housekeeper who turned to her. "I was not aware the young lady was familiar with the family. Certainly."

"Please feel at home." He dipped his head in a smaller bow and then exited the room.

Her breath left her in such a moment of deflation she leaned against the wall for support.

Mary came to stand beside her.

She avoided her gaze, though she knew what she would find there. The same confusion and questions she herself felt. Was she no more than a casual acquaintance to the man? Had he dismissed her already? She dipped her head a moment, staring down at her toes and then made a decision to move forward without further care. She lifted her chin and attempted to find a bit of sparkle to her eyes. "How lovely to offer tea. I do feel that we shall have to decline the kind offer, as we have further engagements this evening."

Her aunt opened her mouth as if to protest, but Lizzie shook her head so she paused. Bless her aunt. Lizzie would have some explaining to do later.

But the group was soon escorted to the front door and after much effusive thanks, Lizzie was at last outside. She breathed deeply the air and then climbed up into the carriage. The sooner they hurried away the better.

What was worse for her? Being completely dismissed by Mr. Darcy as nothing more than a casual acquaintance or being seen at his house, a pathetic and desperate move of a young girl hoping for a bit of his attention?

She couldn't abide the thought of either scenario and both had just happened to her. She clenched her fists together under her skirts, trying to dismiss all thoughts of him from her mind.

"That Darcy is such a polite young man." Mrs. Gardener smiled with appreciation. "He and his brother were both the kindest of humans all growing up. I remember them being loved by all, regular princes for our town, I'll tell you."

"His brother?" Lizzie had not heard of a brother.

"Yes, Arthur and Fitzwilliam. Two peas in a pod so they would say, though I think they are as different as can be."

Lizzie and Mary exchanged a look. Lizzie had heard nothing of any brother.

The carriage made quick work of the return trip and they soon found themselves back in the Inn.

No sooner had they arrived when Mr. Darcy showed up on horseback. He climbed down off his horse and bowed quickly. "I was saddened to hear of your departure. You left without Cook's finest tarts." He offered Lizzie a brown linen package. "She would have nothing but I be about delivering them myself." His half grin was quite charming, and Lizzie found herself even more confused than before. "Thank you." She dipped in another curtsey. "You certainly did not need to do such a thing."

"Oh, you do not know our cook. I most certainly did. And besides, I had hoped to join you."

"You did?" She studied his face. Nothing of the insolence or uncaring appeared there. No concern about her particular family relations. But none of the old familiarity either. Perhaps he was being sincere. Though what to make of this man, she could never know. Would she ever feel completely sure of her reception by him? Somehow she thought she might not. She smiled up into his face. "Again. Thank you. Please send our gratitude to your kind cook as well."

"Of course. And now I must be off." He climbed back up onto his horse and rode away in such a rush that he knocked down a servant carrying a large bag of goods toward the inn.

Without a glance behind him, he continued down the lane at too quick of speed.

Lizzie frowned, and her expression was echoed in all those around her.

She also could not account for his behavior. The Mr. Darcy at the house party would never have behaved so. But the Mr. Darcy in Meryton certainly had. She would never, ever understand this man.

Later that evening, after indulging in far too many delicious chocolate tarts, she could not account for any of it—not for his behavior at any time, really. Who was the man who thought her not handsome enough who then spent particular attention with her at the house party who disrupted the love of her sister Jane who desired to assist her and Lydia in her plight who now behaved in a friendly enough manner but as though they had hardly met? She wasn't certain who this new version of Mr. Darcy could be. She felt so unsettled about him she wasn't certain she could have found a way to thank him if she'd tried. As it was, there had been hardly a moment to say anything at all.

At the early hours of dawn, her eyes finally

closed heavily enough that sleep overtook her tired body and busy mind.

Far too early, while at breakfast, they received a note from Pemberley, delivered by a footman in livery. Lizzie admitted to herself that she felt very fancy as a result. She broke open the seal while the footman waited. Her aunt and each sister in turn stared at her while she perused the contents. She felt her face heat and also felt the gazes of many more in the Inn. She lowered the paper and cleared her throat. "It seems that we have all been invited to dine at Pemberley this evening." Each sister showed different degrees of surprise. Lydia said what they were undoubtedly all—except Mary—thinking.

"Did he not spurn you, Lizzie, and you vowed never to speak his name? I'm glad you are seeing another side to him."

Mary lowered her face in her hands. Lizzie glanced around the room and saw they were perhaps out of earshot of most, but certainly not the footman who was trained well enough to show no reaction to Lydia's comment.

"On the contrary, we spent time at a house

party this spring and are indeed on better terms..." A long-shared gaze with Mary did not clear her thoughts. "Though things are certainly odd." She turned to the footman. "I do believe we will accept. Send our regards and gratitude."

He nodded, bowed, and turned to leave.

As soon as he was out of earshot, Mary turned to Lydia. "Surely you could have kept your opinions to yourself in front of the footman."

Mrs. Gardener placed a hand over Mary's. "Your sister is correct, but I do think Lizzie recovered quickly and all will be well."

Lizzie stared at the missive. *"I request the honor of your presence in my home this evening for dinner. Please don't deny me this privilege."* She mused within herself and could not fathom what day she would begin to understand Mr. Darcy. It was certainly not yesterday or this day or any other day she had yet known him. He behaved in wildly erratic ways, one day knowing her well enough to ask how to help in a highly personal situation, interfering in her sister's happiness, and then the next acting as though they were barely acquaintances. And in fact, appeared as though he might want to pursue her? Her face colored further and she did not know what else to do besides attend dinner at Pemberley and see what manner of the man called Mr. Darcy she would meet that evening.

CHAPTER 20
ELIZABETH

T hey went for a walk through town. They had not yet seen all the shops, and Aunt was looking forward to reconnecting with many families and friends. Kitty ran straight for the milliners, and soon the sisters were gathered round bonnets and bits of ribbon. Mary found a corner of the store with a few books for sale, and Lizzie wandered out to the street where she was soon drawn in by the sounds of children chanting their maths.

She followed the sound across the street and peered in the window of what looked like a school room. A young lady stood at the front. She was light like Lizzie's sister Jane, with rosy cheeks and a light in her face and eyes that immediately made Lizzie smile. She was perhaps one of the most wholesome pictures Lizzie had yet seen. The lady noticed Lizzie's face outside the window and beckoned her inside.

As soon as she stepped in the room, the teacher smiled at her students. "Please continue practicing with the person next to you. Let me welcome our visitor."

The children watched for a moment with open curiosity but soon turned to their partners and began practicing.

Lizzie nodded in approval. "They are lovely."

"They really are. The villagers have not had much of an education unless we who live here teach them what we can. They are more grateful than anything." She smiled so fondly at the backs of their heads that Lizzie was immediately endeared to this new woman.

"I was so drawn to the sounds of their excited maths." She laughed. "I guess I couldn't resist being that face in the window."

"Are you here long? I will be sending them off for lunch in just a moment. Would you like to get a bite with me?"

"Yes, very much." Lizzie moved to the back of the room to watch but she waved her over.

"I could use the assistance if you still know your figures?"

Lizzie laughed and nodded. "I help my father with the books sometimes."

"Oh, that is impressive indeed, and more than I do. I'm not sure my brother would appreciate me anywhere near the books. He barely allows my other brother a moment in them, and he's the heir." She shrugged, and while Lizzie tried to figure out what she could mean by that, the woman pointed to the boy on the third row. "Could you start there with him?"

"Of course." Lizzie crouched down at his side and began helping him work through the numbers on his board.

Lizzie enjoyed herself so much she decided that if marriage never worked for her, she could be happy indeed as a governess.

As soon as the children were out the door and off to whatever they did during their lunch, the teacher linked arms with Lizzie. "Now, I am Miss Georgiana. And we must stop in at Penny's Bakery, if you don't mind. I don't think I can last the rest of the day without a crumpet."

Lizzie laughed. "Then we must go to Penny's. It's lovely to meet you. I'm Miss Elizabeth. My friends call me Lizzie, which I hope you will as well."

"Lizzie it is then, as I hope to always be Georgiana."

They continued to walk arm in arm with Lizzie feeling the warmth of new friendship and a bit of happy surprise at finding someone she so quickly enjoyed.

They moved down the street to Penny's and as soon as Lizzie stepped in the door, she knew she had made an excellent decision. The room smelled of freshly baked scones. The warmth of chocolate and toffee filled the air, and a smiley-faced woman stepped to the counter the minute the door closed behind them.

"Why, Miss Georgiana, I hope those children aren't giving you any trouble."

"Not at all. They are lovely as always. Your Leroy did exceptionally well with his numbers today. Miss Elizabeth assisted for a moment."

"Oh yes, he picked it up so quickly."

"Glad I am to hear it. He's a smart one, if he would just apply himself." She clucked. "Now, what can I get you today? Anything you like as a thank you. I can't explain how much it means to us that you'd be willing to try and teach our children." She dabbed her eyes with her towel which was covered in flour. Georgiana's mouth twitched and Lizzie bit back a laugh. She was the perfect picture of a baker—down to a smudge of flour on the face.

They both ordered, and as they gathered their sweets—including some wrapped items Georgiana was bringing home to her brother and housekeeper—Penny leaned across the counter. "Your brother is doing good by us all to put that scoundrel behind bars. There is nothing at all good that can come of such a man free to ruin the lives of good women everywhere. Not to mention the debt he racked up all over Derbyshire. Grateful I will always be for your family." She pressed a hand to her heart. And then the door opened, so she straightened and greeted the new guests.

Lizzie glanced curiously at Georgiana but she seemed to be more reserved. The news was certainly having an effect. They ate a few bites of an admittedly delicious crumpet and then Georgiana sighed. "I must apologize for my wool gathering. You must have noticed. That news of my brother and the man he is putting behind bars... I feel personally affected by it."

"I, too, know a man who almost ruined my sister and us all. So you will hear no judgment from me. If it helps to talk about it, I will keep your secrets," Lizzie replied.

She shifted a moment. "My brother has recently learned of terrible actions of a man we all grew up with. He abducted a young girl, left a bunch of unanswered debt all over town, and it seemed had no intention of marrying the girl." She shook a moment. And then rubbed her hands up and down her arms. "But Fitz found him and presented evidence against him and he will be shipped off and exiled, never to harm another soul in England again." Her lips quivered. "He convinced me once of his love. I thought myself equally in love." She looked away. "How foolish."

Lizzie reached for her hand. "No. That doesn't make you foolish. The ability to love and to love deeply is a gift. And you are not at fault for loving someone who was imperfect. I'm terribly sad someone so undeserving was the recipient of your love."

She shook her head. "No. It wasn't really him I loved. How could it be, since I was mistaken about who he was. It was the idea of who I thought he was. Gallant, kind, caring, ready to place me at the center of their universe." She fiddled with her food. "Sounds foolish now."

Lizzie felt her eyes fill with tears. Shocked at her own emotional reaction, she waved a hand in front of her face. "Oh my goodness. But no. You are anything but foolish. The worst parts about this whole situation are these feelings left inside you. I wish there was a way to ban them from your heart." She wished the same for Lydia. Perhaps it would be good for the two to meet. She sat back in her chair. "Do you think a man such as you imagined really exists? Is there such a person?"

Georgiana lifted one corner of her mouth and Lizzie was pleased to see some cheer returning to her new friend.

"I have a brother who is just like that. Maybe two." She laughed.

"Maybe?"

"Well, yes, two. One is more reliable and one is more...spontaneous."

Lizzie laughed. "I wonder what you aren't saying there?" She took a sip of tea. "But which one worked to put the bad man in jail?"

"The spontaneous one. Actually they both did."

Lizzie nodded. "So they both have good hearts."

"Oh definitely. I think so." She dabbed her mouth. "This has been so lovely. I do believe I'm going to miss you. But I have to return to my class."

"Oh yes! And my sisters and aunt are here in town somewhere as well."

"Goodness, I have kept you." Georgiana looked terribly sorry.

But Lizzie shook her head. "Oh dear, no. I've kept myself. Time well spent. I'm pleased to meet you."

"And I you. I'll invite you for tea once I get our schedule from the brothers. I believe they are coming into town."

Lizzie smiled. "I'd like that."

She watched Georgiana walk out the bakery door. What could have happened with this particularly terrible man? She shook her head, mumbling to herself. Dear Lydia. Dear every woman at the mercy of men like Wickham. Some were very lucky and still able to have a life of some normalcy. Others would never again be able to join proper Society. Worse still, others were tied to such a man in marriage. Lizzie shuddered.

And yet, Miss Georgiana was lucky indeed to have brothers such as hers. Lizzie smiled to herself. Her thoughts turned to Mr. Darcy. Had he too been their savior? Had he rescued Lydia and then protected everyone from Wickham?

She felt a sudden tightness in her throat and moisture at her eyes. How did one thank a person for such an act? She would certainly try at dinner this evening. He was a puzzle and certainly difficult to converse with. But perhaps dinner would lend itself to a moment of quiet conversation.

She exited out on the street in time to see a carriage ride too quickly through town, hit a puddle, and completely douse a young boy with dirty water.

"Oh no!" She ran out to him.

His little lips quivered. Muddy water streamed down his face.

"You poor dear." The small handkerchief she produced and used to at least wipe his eyes and mouth did little to help with anything else. It was soon a darker brown than he. "And where do you belong, little man?"

His eyes twinkled with a bit of mischief. "I shoulda been in school just now. Wouldna gotten hit by the Darcy carriage if I'da just been sitting in class with Miss Georgiana." He shrugged.

"Well, let's walk you there now, shall we?" She pressed her lips together. "Are you certain it was the Darcy carriage?"

He nodded. "That Mr. Darcy thinks it's a bit of a game."

"Does he, now?" Her steps altered themselves to match her mood and resembled more of a stomp than the delicate placing of feet of most ladies.

By the time she arrived at the school door, she had quite forgotten the warm feelings toward a man who found it amusing to treat young people so.

The carriage returned just as she opened the door. It was again moving way too quickly, and a group of women scurried out of the way to avoid being trampled by the horses.

She could feel herself tightening up.

Her wave to Georgiana was briefer than

before and with an air of irritation but she paused a moment for a warmer smile. It was not as though her new friend owned that carriage.

Mr. Darcy was long gone when she stepped back out onto the street. But her thoughts were not. Her sisters exited the bakery just then and waved to her.

Kitty ran toward her. "Oh Lizzie, that is the most scrumptious place. You must try nearly everything they make."

She laughed in spite of her irritation and then linked arms with Kitty. "Must I? What is your favorite sweet?"

She tried to douse her irritation with Darcy while getting another tour of the bakery, this time from Kitty. Was there a way she could possibly avoid attending dinner hosted by a man she could not respect?

Unless she became violently ill, she was likely to be compelled to go. She could never offend those at Pemberley, particularly not when accompanying her aunt who loved this area and grew up admiring all in the house.

The best she could do was try to distract her mind with anything else until she was forced to think once again about the man.

CHAPTER 21
ARTHUR DARCY

For many miles, Darcy rode slowly toward his aunt's home, Rosings Park, his mount restlessly trying to move faster than a slow walk, but with Darcy holding him back. Both rider and mount were unhappy with the situation. The carriage followed at whatever pace he set. Darcy did a lot of things he did not want to do. He was always putting duty before just about everything in his life. So why was this redirection to his aunt's house in Kent such an inconvenience to him? Not just an inconvenience; he was dreading it. He pressed a thumb on the bridge of his nose. Why could his brother not simply do what he was asked? Darcy's lip twitched. Because it was not Arthur's place to be telling the heir of Pemberley how to behave. How many hours had he spent wishing his brother would simply take over and fulfill his responsibilities well? And now that he was wishing to be home—and hopefully taking an interest—Arthur should be celebrating.

But it didn't feel quite like Fitz was taking it all on. He felt more like Fitz was sloughing off what seemed unpleasant to him for his brother to handle. And that was the problem. For one of the few moments in Arthur's life, he seriously considered going to Pemberley anyway. His aunt would be just fine. She had a capable steward. And last he heard, his cousin Anne was in moderately good health. He pulled up on the reins. There was quite a long list of things Darcy would rather do than his brother's bidding at Rosings. Miss Elizabeth's smiling mouth came into his mind unbidden. He would very much like to pay a visit to the beautiful Miss Elizabeth. He'd like to stay at his own estate. Since meeting Miss Elizabeth, he was more and more restless about Pemberley and more desirous to spend time where he would be building his own legacy, where he would be building a family, where his wife would be. Again, Miss Elizabeth overtook his thoughts. He was certainly not finished with her. He wasn't certain he ever would be. She had overtaken his thoughts, his heart function, and had seized full control of his ability to smile.

Without bidding, his lips curled up. He shook his head. She had bewitched him. And he wasn't certain what to do about it.

Should he turn and head to Longbourne?

He was itching to do so. His feet were about ready to urge his horse exactly there when he heard the galloping of hooves coming toward him.

Instinctively, he moved to the side but sat tall in his seat.

The rider pulled up. "I'm looking for a gentleman, Mr. Darcy."

"You have found me."

The man reached in his pocket to hand Arthur a note, with the Darcy family seal. "Are you awaiting a response?"

"Yes, sir, I am." He dipped his head.

Darcy broke the seal and scanned the letter quickly. "No need to respond. I suspect I'll ride faster than you. Take a break, man." He reached for coins to give to the man.

He smiled. "My thanks to you then."

"Certainly." His brother was now summoning him back to Pemberley. He would be annoyed but instead the smile that filled his face might have cracked it. He was heading home. And from there, he could then visit Long-bourne. And what was more? His brother mentioned a lady. Could it be that he was at last attempting to settle down? The fact that he'd written of tenant difficulties was encouraging. He'd never showed an interest in them before, even though they were the greatest source of the Darcy income.

He raced back in the direction of Pemberley. He'd need to head straight for the families involved. There had been flooding and a small dispute between residents as well as some family need, sickness. He'd care for them first and then find his way to a hot bath.

While he raced along the mostly deserted roads to Pemberley, the rhythm of his horse beneath him felt calming. It was the only sound he could hear, and his breathing matched every second set of feet falling on the earth. Things began to feel more clear. He would move into his own estate. He'd set up his rooms there. He would finish the renovations while living there himself. It was time to tell his brother that Pemberley was his.

Thoughts of the tenant families came immediately to mind. But Darcy nodded to himself. Fitz could take care of it. If he knew he was the only hope for someone, he would rise to the occasion. Look what happened with the Wickham situation. He had notion of Arthur's prior involvement and took matters into his capable hands. Wickham was now shipped off to Australia. Fitz was ready.

This woman he mentioned briefly showed promise. He had said something about her not being easily swayed. That he would need to work for her good will.

Darcy grinned. "Good show, woman, whoever you are."

His horse snorted.

He patted his neck. "Good show to you as well. We'll be home soon, old boy."

Racing through the fields and on the roads to his childhood home, he knew that if Miss Elizabeth would have him, she too would not be easily swayed. He wasn't certain exactly why she had been so resistant to him, why she thought he'd ruined a sister's happiness. But she was not one to fawn or swoon over a man, he presumed, and certainly not over him. But perhaps there was something he could do to win that heart of hers, something that would prove he was not whatever she dreaded she might find in a man.

He was soon riding through the back lands of his estate. There was indeed mud everywhere and signs of flooding, when he rounded the bend; the devastation in front of him stole his breath.

Had his brother gone to assess the damage himself? Did he know the situation? He guessed not, else servants from the household, people from town, any others, the vicar himself would surely be in attendance.

He leapt off his horse, his boots sinking a bit in the mud. "Stay close, old boy." He patted Samson. The first house, the home of the Gallaghers, had mud piled up at the door, basically trapping them inside. He could hear the sounds of people. The windows might have offered an escape, but from the sounds, there were still some inside. "Hello in the house. Hello."

A haggard, mud-streaked face appeared in the window. "Oh, is it you, Mr. Darcy?"

"It is I, Mrs. Gallagher. I do believe we need to get you out of there."

She looked down at the ground beneath her. "Has the water subsided, then?"

"It has, but the mud has not. It is certainly not an easy passage. But I can carry you to the rise over there?" He pointed up the road to the top of the bend.

She nodded. "And where shall we go?" A shaking hand brushed the hair from her face. "I think there are folks worse off than we. Should we stay put, then?"

He shook his head. "I don't think so. I think instead we might be having many more guests looking for a bit of floor and a dry place to be? We don't have beds for one and all but we do have space."

"Oh dear me no, we can't be staying at the great house. We will find a spot at the church, surely."

"Why don't we discover the situations of all and see what would be best?"

She nodded.

"And how are your young ones?"

"They're cold. But we are huddling together in the blankets."

"Do you have a shovel or a bit of wood or something I can use to scrape away this mud?"

"David took that with him to help up the road. Hours ago." A child started whimpering in the background. She hesitated.

"Go help your child. Maybe you will all pass through the window here. Do you think you can manage if I help you on this side?"

She looked behind her, seemingly assessing. Then she nodded. "I think so. It would be nice to get warm." She rubbed her arms. "But, Mr. Darcy, you're going to be covered in mud! Surely the servants have been alerted." She looked past him as if someone else might be coming to assist as well.

"I don't know if anyone else has been alerted. I came straight here. But we shall free you of your cold, wet prison, shall we?"

She nodded. "Thank you. Thank you with all our hearts."

Darcy found a bit of an old tree and started pulling away at the dirt at their front door. It was cold and thick, like clay, up against the wood. The walls seemed thin. The wood was solid, there were no holes, but at the same time, he wondered if he had been neglecting the tenants even while thinking he'd taken such good care. They were cold without a fire and easily trapped inside from the mud.

Mrs. Gallagher reappeared at the window, the top part of her oldest lad's head visible next to her. "I have Leroy here. He can help with the young'uns out there."

"He's a hefty lad, if I remember, but I can get him if you give a little boost from your side."

She tried to grab him round the middle but he shook his head. "No, Mama. You cup your hands like Pa. I'll stand on them and then Mr. Darcy, beggin' your pardon, sir, but he will catch me on the outside."

"He's exactly right and no apologies. We are all working together here. And there are more to help down the lane, I gather."

"We think so, Mr. Darcy, sir." His little head bobbed as though nodding yes. Soon he was fully visible and starting to climb out the window. Darcy reached for him and pulled him through.

Soon they were each out and standing slightly up the road on a dry spot. But now what to do with them? No cart would be able to navigate these roads and paths very well. And from the looks of things, many more would need assistance. He'd best be walking back toward the house and then enlisting the servants and sending word to the town and the vicar.

He whistled for his horse who had not gone far. But when he approached the small family with Samson at his side, they all crouched away in fear.

"Oh, Mr. Darcy. I don't know about him." Mrs. Gallagher clutched her baby to her. The younger one clung to her skirts, and Leroy stood close by. He seemed the least worried but was still not comfortable by any stretch.

"He's very obedient." He patted his side. "Would you like to touch him?"

The horse shuffled his feet right then, likely a bit unnerved by their fear.

"Whoa, boy." He rubbed his nose. But the horse seemed unsettled.

He nodded. "Looks like we might be walking." He turned to Mrs. Gallagher. "Can you do so?"

"We can try." She looked back to her home. "Should we try to send word to David?"

"We should. But let's get you back first and I'll send a lot more than word."

She paused a moment more and then nodded. "Let's be off, then. Children. Be strong. We have a lot of walking to do with good Mr. Darcy."

He crouched down to the little one at her skirts. "Could I put you on my shoulders, little one?"

Leroy nodded. "Yes, Frankie. Mr. Darcy is a real good one."

Frankie hesitated a moment but then smiled and nodded.

Within moments Darcy and Frankie, Mrs. Gallagher and the baby, and Leroy were walking the path back to the house with Samson following a short distance behind. It was not going to be the shortest walk of their lives but at least they weren't miles and miles away.

When they at last approached the house, Darcy had the baby in his arms as well as Frankie on his shoulders. The lad was clutching his hair in handfuls. Mrs. Gallagher had a good hold of Leroy's hand and steadied herself on his shoulder now and again. "We are at last approaching." He breathed out some of his worry in a great sense of relief. The back doors opened and servants came flooding out.

"Oh, Mr. Darcy!" Their housekeeper was a gem of a woman, and she immediately reached for the baby. "Mrs. Gallagher, come inside. You all must warm yourselves."

Darcy thanked her and then asked, "Please. Where is my brother?"

"In the main dining room, if it please you." The maid who answered bobbed a curtsey and took Frankie into her arms.

He made his way directly to the dining room. Perhaps more care could be taken with the floors and the mud that undeniably made its way into the house, but he was in a hurry and he needed to get things moving...and he wished to share a few words with his brother who was apparently at dinner.

He waved away the footmen who moved as though to open doors and announce him. But as soon as he stepped into the room, he could see why they were standing on formality that evening.

Everyone in the room stood.

And everyone looked quite amazed as they stared at him.

Miss Elizabeth was perhaps more stunning than he had yet seen her. And he couldn't account for her presence, nor for her seat to the right of his brother, nor for the presence of all her sisters. He opened his mouth and then closed it twice before shaking his head. "Brother?"

Miss Elizabeth looked from one to the other in great confusion.

Georgiana's eyes sparkled with amusement as she brought a hand to her mouth. "Arthur..." She pointed up to his hair. He belatedly remembered Frankie's fistfuls of hair surely restyling his in an unrecognizable manner.

"Arthur?" Miss Elizabeth turned to his brother. "And forgive me. You're Fitzwilliam?"

"I am." He dipped his head. "I should introduce you to the final Darcy sibling. This is my brother Arthur."

She nodded, swallowed once and then curtseyed. "You're twins."

"Yes, we are. I..." Fitz looked from Miss Elizabeth to Arthur and back. "Are you two acquainted?"

She gripped her hands together at her front and exchanged a look with Miss Mary then she turned to Georgiana. She pointed to Fitz. "The spontaneous one?"

She nodded.

Fitz tilted his head as if to ask something of Georgiana but paused.

Arthur cleared his throat. "I would love to join you." He held out his hands at the delicious spread. "And please forgive me, Miss Elizabeth, Miss Mary, Miss Lydia, and the other sisters whom I have not met. But we are having a dire situation with the tenants. Fitz. This is hardly the time for you to be so inclined..." He turned to Miss Elizabeth again. "Please forgive my abrupt entrance and now exit." He turned to leave. "Brother."

But Miss Elizabeth hurried toward him from the table. "Please no. We can help. What is the dire situation? There is no need for us to be sitting at dinner when others are in need."

"Are you quite certain? I must look a sight. There is mud, and very few solutions besides walking through it."

"I am certain, of course. Have you boots in the barn?"

His mouth lifted of its own volition and he chuckled. "We do indeed."

"Then I shall try to be of assistance." Miss Elizabeth's eyes shone with a fire he could hardly resist. He stepped closer, her gaze nearly swallowing him whole.

Her expression softened and she whispered, "It is the least I can do after you have done so much."

"I know you did not ask for assistance, but I suspected I knew where they'd gone. I had to help. I hope...you were not? Offended?"

She shook her head.

They were close now, closer than he intended but he could not resist her nearness. Her lovely smell of mint and cloves and lavender, the softness and fullness of her lips. She was so much more than he even remembered, and to see her in his childhood home, hear her so willing to assist in a task very much unlike anything most ladies were accustomed... He raised his hand as though to touch her face.

Fitz cleared his throat.

Arthur all but jumped back. She'd been sitting by his brother. He'd mentioned a young lady... His heart filled with dread.

But Miss Elizabeth did not seem at all uncomfortable with him. She turned. "We shall discuss later why no one mentioned you were a twin? And I would be most interested to know with whom I have been conversing and when... though now that I see you together, I have my guesses."

Miss Mary's eyes twinkled with amusement, as did Georgiana's. He shook his head. "It promises to be very diverting, at the least. Now, if you'll come with me to the kitchen. I've asked the servants to gather." He paused and turned to his sister. "Could you please coordinate the help here with the others? We will have great need. Many will come to spend the night. Perhaps in the great hall? We need fires roaring. Food from the kitchen, blankets..."

Georgiana waved him off. "I understand, brother. We will handle things from here. I'm certain with Mrs. Gardiner and the Bennet sisters, as well as our own capable staff, we will have things well in line. If anyone comes looking for news, what shall I direct them to do?"

"Like the vicar? Please send any capable hands to the tenant farmers, particularly the row off Periwinkle Lane."

She nodded. The other Bennet sisters stepped forward along with their aunt. He smiled. "Thank you. There is much good we can do. And you are helping me save the estate.

What are we without the tenants?" He waited for his brother and Miss Elizabeth to join him and then he made his way toward the barn. His conversation with Fitz about many things would have to wait until later. Miss Elizabeth moved to walk beside him but Fitz stepped between them.

Yes, they had much to discuss, indeed.

CHAPTER 22
ELIZABETH

Lizzie's mind was a storm. Not just wind and rain but a torrential, tropical, dangerous storm. With swells and circular motions and blasts of rain and sudden quiet. She was not exactly unhappy. She was confused. She was unsure. And through the midst of it all, she was very happy.

But also hesitant.

Realizing that all the things that had bothered her about Mr. Darcy were not in fact found in one of the twins, that she'd treated him abominably for no reason at all except that she'd met his twin, and knowing that certainly she'd never put her best self forward to a man who was undeniably suddenly so attractive to her she was finding it difficult to breathe, she wasn't certain how to move forward.

She was aware of every fall of his mud-covered boots. Even though Fitz walked between them, a heart-pounding heat and energy flowed in her direction through or around the brother. She could hardly think, hardly walk on her own. She placed a hand at her heart.

Fitz immediately turned to her. "Are you well? Should we adjust our pace?" Fitz frowned at Arthur. "Sometimes the task at hand becomes more important than the people performing it around here."

Arthur shook his head, but he turned to her with concern. "Are we moving too quickly? The barn is just up ahead…"

She shook her head. "No, I'm fine. I have much on my mind that is quite exhilarating and I have to admit, stealing my breath." Her eyes sought his. She could not resist her subtle declarations. She could not resist him at all. He stepped closer. "I, too, have much on my mind."

Fitz again cleared his throat. "Perhaps we should continue then, if everyone is able to keep the breakneck speed of my brother's walking pace."

"Yes, I'm well."

"Well, indeed."

Fitz moved forward, returning to their previous pace. Lizzie fell in step with Arthur so that now she was walking between the twins.

The heat burning off of him almost jumped out to her.

Twice, their hands brushed and even through her gloves, she found it tingly and exhilarating and full of yearning. More. She wanted more of him, more brushing, more nearness, more of him.

She knew he might not be hers. She knew he might not care for her, and he'd have every reason to think her quite the harpy, if she were being honest. But she could in no way shield her heart anymore from this man. He was truly all that she'd wanted. Now that the previous concerns were put to rest, she felt free to love him. But steady on, she would need to pace herself.

Ridiculous, desperate craving was not something she thought she'd ever feel. But at the moment that's all she could feel. She needed to overcome this or else she'd make a bumbling fool of herself for the rest of the day.

Fitz hummed to himself a moment and then stopped. "I met you in Meryton."

She and Arthur both paused as well, Arthur pressing his lips together.

She nodded. "Yes, that was you." She laughed and turned to Arthur. "And it was you at the house party."

"House party?" Fitz tilted his head.

"Lord Shackley invited us both, with Miss Mary as well."

"And that is where you two met." Fitz rubbed his chin with his hand. "But you thought I was him?"

"I thought you were both the same person this whole time."

"That must have been a bit of a turmoil." Fitz nodded.

"Yes, to say the least. You two did not treat me the same way..."

"Then I can only blame myself for my behavior in Meryton not to immediately notice the diamond in that small town and do all in my power to be more impressive of a catch." He winked. Before she could respond, he pointed toward the barn. "Shall we be off, then?"

"Yes, we shall." Arthur softened his tone

with a gentle smile to them both. "Though I, too, am very intrigued in all that happened between the two of you while she thought it was I."

"Or she thought you were I." Fitz pointed.

She laughed. "This is quite a story. And I'm surprised it doesn't happen more often."

"Well, most often, we are near people who already know us or at least know of us. Meryton is not somewhere we have ever been."

As they approached the barn, servants opened the doors and stood at attention. She'd never experienced anything like the fineness of Pemberley.

Arthur glanced in her direction once more and then stepped forward. "We are going to need as many as can possibly be spared to assist on Periwinkle Lane. The flood has trapped many, and I don't know the situations of others. Our home is open. The vicarage, I'm assuming, is as well. Perhaps we will need the barn. Please grab warm blankets and carts and make your way to assist."

They immediately sprang into action. Arthur himself opened the stores and grabbed a handful of blankets.

Fitzwilliam turned to her. "And someone

needs to take care of you." He called to a passing servant. "Could we get a pair of boots for the lady?"

"Yes, very good, sir."

"Thank you. I do hope to be of use. I can't imagine being flooded in my own home."

"Nor I." He shuddered. "But they are more used to it than we, I would assume. Don't allow yourself to be overcome. They will be well."

"Yes, thanks to your family. It's wonderful how you treat them." She remembered his recklessness in town. "I only feel sorry that you felt the need to entertain us while so many suffered. We would have understood had you needed to cancel or leave us, or anything at all." She watched him.

His face remained blank. But he toyed with his timepiece for a moment. "My brother and I see things differently. I, of course, knew that the tenants were in trouble. The vicar is working. The tenants themselves are working. I alerted Arthur. And I had important guests at my table. All in good time, everything can be taken care of." He held her gaze a moment longer. "I don't think anything is more important than your time at my table or that of your family."

His words shook her to the core. Powerful sentiments she could not help but be affected by coursed through her like her life force. Did she feel the same? Would she have cared enough about her guests to be certain they were the most important for at least the time they were in her home? Did this Darcy twin actually care for her?

She saw only sincerity in his expression.

"I know we have not been able to converse much at all, but I was hoping this evening to express an interest, to show you my earnest desire to know you better." He sighed. "But, naturally, my brother feels something along those lines and I sense you might?"

A servant arrived with the boots, saving Lizzie from responding just yet.

Fitz indicated a bench against the wall. "Might I assist you?"

"Yes, thank you." She studied his face. It was the same face she'd looked at countless times, sometimes as Fitz and sometimes as Arthur. But she could see the differences now. It was mostly in expressions, but Fitz was definitely Fitz, and he had a softer, sincere side she was appreciating greatly at the moment. Seems as though, once you impressed the man, he was all yours. At least for a time. She rested a hand on his arm. "Who knows what would have happened had I been handsome enough to tempt you." She laughed.

He groaned and rubbed a hand over his face.

"But I hold no ill feelings. Sometimes things happen for a reason."

"Is there no hope of convincing you still? No pull of Pemberley itself? We might not yet have an affection but surely you can see all that would be available here." His eyes held hope.

And she couldn't dash that hope, but she couldn't inflame it further, either. "I do love Pemberley already. And the opportunity to do so much good. But I want a marriage of more than convenience."

She sat and he lifted one of her feet. "Then I shall have to win your heart or give in to a brother who has perhaps already won it?" He studied her face that she tried to keep from turning bright red, with little success. He ran his thumb over the side of her ankle. "With your permission?"

She nodded. No man had ever touched her

feet before. Was this permitted? She glanced down the barn to find Arthur.

He was surrounded by servants and seemed to be organizing the rescue effort, or at least to have forgotten all about them.

She was about to nod her consent when Arthur glanced their way. He held up a hand and hurried in their direction. "Fitz. They are in need of your direction. Could you lead the first group? They need your exceptional abilities with horses. I think I can assist Miss Elizabeth from here, and we will move with the second group." He was standing in front of them in what seemed to be two strides, his hand outstretched as if to ask for the boot in Fitz's.

She felt her mouth drop and forced it closed. The two stood eye-to-eye, and she recognized just how identical they were, the same height, same jaw line, same handsome features. But there was a tenderness to Arthur that seemed more of an edge in Fitz, and even the strength displayed by Arthur in his commands was the kind of leadership that people wanted to follow. Fitz might be intimidating in some settings, but he would not often be admired, at least not yet.

She saw so much potential in him, but Arthur seemed to have already arrived.

Goodness. The power of two Darcies both vying for her attention was almost too much. She stood. "I think I can don my own boot, but thank you very much for the offers to assist." She tucked both boots under her arm and moved farther down in the barn to a different bench.

Fitz and Arthur engaged in a rapid-fire conversation which she would have loved to overhear but dare not.

After what seemed an eternity, both brothers gripped the other's shoulder and Fitz moved toward the group of servants hard at work, preparing to leave by loading carts with needed supplies. After a few steps, he turned to Lizzie and dipped his head in a half bow.

She smiled her encouragement and then Arthur stood in front of her. He knelt. "I see you've made no progress with your boot." His smile was soft, tender and his eyes sparkling with light and admiration.

"I have not." Her face colored. "I find my mind is highly engaged in the mystery of two Darcys when I thought there was only one."

He closed his eyes. "When I met you at the house party..."

"I thought you were Fitz."

"And he was less than gentlemanly?"

She looked away, not wishing to speak ill of him. "I... He did not seem to favor my company." She gasped. "Nor that of my sister nor her relationship with Bingley." She placed a hand over her mouth. "Oh, Mr. Darcy. I have treated you so ill. I must apologize."

He reached for her foot. "May I?"

Her mouth went dry but she nodded and lifted her foot so that it fit in his hand. His large, strong fingers slipped the slipper off of her foot, placing it on the bench beside her. One hand cupped her foot, his fingers gently rubbing against the skin at her ankle while the other lifted the boot. "I do think this will fit well enough. It is not, perhaps, the prettiest of feet adornments." He laughed as a large and clunky but very useful boot encased her foot and leg up to her knee.

"I shall fully appreciate these, I'm certain, as we go slogging in the mud."

"You will, indeed."

He lifted her other foot, both hands cradling its stocking smallness. "You have lovely feet."

Her smile turned to a soft laugh. "I don't think I ever imagined such a compliment."

"Oh? And what do you think of it now that it is received?" His smile widened.

"I find you might say all manner of compliments and I would never tire of them." She forced herself not to look away, though she felt more bold than she'd ever been.

"Then I shall find many reasons to shower them upon you, for I've been thinking them up these many long weeks."

"You have?"

"I most certainly have. And trying with no avail to forget them."

"Oh dear."

"You were clearly not interested in hearing them then."

"Not from Fitz...but from you? You are an entirely different opportunity."

He squeezed her ankle one more time and then slid on the clunky boot. "And now, my lady, we are off to the tenants. I'm afraid it will not be the beautiful house tour, nor the quiet parlor game or the boisterous charades but rather, the smudged and dirty faces of cold and wet people in need." He was not apologizing.

And she was smiling even wider. "I shall enjoy it far more than anything else we could do together, I do believe."

He laughed with his belly then which made her join him, though she had no idea the cause of such amusement.

"Then you, my dear, will be delightful to please." He reached for her hands and brought her to stand in front of him. "I can promise you one thing."

"Only one?" She widened her eyes, glued to his face to hear what it might be.

"Only one for now." He shook his head. "I cannot believe this is actually happening right now."

"Nor I. I shall not sleep tonight. This seems but a dream." She stepped nearer, without even thinking. "But what is the thing you promise?"

"Oh yes, I promise that we shall do other more enjoyable things than rescue the tenants."

"What a lovely thought. How many?"

"How many things?"

"Yes, I shall have to clear my calendar." She tapped her chin.

"A lifetime of them, if you can find the time." His face colored slightly and then he held out his arm. "But enough of that before I go making a muddle of things before they can even begin. Shall we?"

She placed her hand at his elbow. "We shall, most definitely, begin."

He rested a hand on top of hers. "I've instructed the servants to take you back to the house at the first sign of real fatigue."

"What?" She stopped and turned to him. "We shall have none of that."

"I cannot have you working yourself to exhaustion."

"I will not overly tax myself. But I will be tired. I love a good tired, don't you? The kind where you fall into bed knowing you did something of worth that day."

"Keep talking, Miss Elizabeth, and I won't ever be able to let you go."

She was quiet for so long after that, in awe and wonder that Mr. Arthur Darcy could speak so to her, that he paused their steps. "Have I scared you already?"

"Oh my goodness, no. I'm merely trying to exercise a bit of restraint over here."

"And what are you restraining, might I ask?" His eyebrow twitched with a sort of wicked gleam, but she laughed and shook her head. "Oh no. I shall not reveal such things yet. There is still a mystery to unfold. That is part of the fun, is it not?"

"It most definitely is. And I shall enjoy every smallest bit I unravel."

Her face warmed so much she felt feverish. "And now we shall have to pretend once again to be at odds."

"Why would we do that?" He frowned.

"So we can accomplish something this evening." She laughed. "I would certainly like to be of use."

"And we shall." He waved to a servant who stepped forward. "Our conveyance awaits." They rounded a corner, and a cart full of supplies was loaded and ready with a donkey to pull it.

"Most excellent." She circled around to climb in, but Mr. Darcy called out.

"Now wait. I must help you up like a gentleman should."

"Ah, very true." She placed her hand in his and the thrill of any attention from him raced through her. "I don't suppose I shall get used to that too quickly."

"Did you enjoy that as much as I?"

"I might have." She grinned. "Now stop. We are not to flirt so shamelessly."

"Ah, success! If you noticed I'm flirting, I'm at last doing it correctly."

She laughed, with abandon. "You are too self-deprecating. I'm certain there are many women half in love with you and your charms."

He shook his head gravely. "I have not wished to know many women in such a manner. I'm generally much more reserved. Some call me proud."

She studied him for a few minutes and just nodded. "But I'd think it was a good kind of pride. I cannot imagine the arrogance on the faces of so many on you. It wouldn't fit."

His eyes twinkled, and he took the reins. "And now we are off."

They moved out down the lane. "Where are we headed?"

"We are in search of the vicar. First stop, the vicarage. I do believe he is hosting many there, and he will have news on the rest, I hope."

"And Fitz?"

Darcy's eyes clouded a moment, but he smiled. "My brother will assist those who have been left or trapped or unreachable from the vicarage but more accessible from our side of the dirt trails."

"Is that where you found the others?"

"Yes, it was. And a sad state they were in."

She nodded. "We shall do all we can. I admit to being anxious to arrive."

"I, too. But I will not begrudge a moment or two with you. Of all the pursuits today, even though some are, indeed, very pressing, my pursuit of you is the most important to me. I hope you know that. Even though things will get drastically busy and I may leave or be distracted, this right here is where I long to be."

She nodded. "I would not want you to stay too close if it meant others could not be helped, though my heart might wish otherwise." Her face flamed. She was so bold. She had never been this bold. But he seemed to listen with supreme contentment as though she brought him great balms of comfort.

"We will make a good pair this night then, I suspect."

CHAPTER 23
ARTHUR

They arrived at the vicarage, and things were much worse than he expected. Everyone was in good spirits, more or less, but they were overtaking the vicarage with nowhere else to rest. And more kept coming. Families were sitting about on the lawn. And the night air had grown more chill.

Miss Elizabeth's eyes filled with tears. "This is so much. These poor people."

"Yes, we must bring them to the great house."

"You are so good, so generous."

He lifted her hand to his mouth, heart in his throat to see her so affected by the plight of others. "We must. We will help them be safe and comfortable. And then we must work to repair the roads."

"Oh dear. How shall all of them make their way? Do we have carts enough?"

"I don't know if carts are the best solution. But I suppose we can shuttle back and forth with the carts."

"The carriage would be stuck in all this mud, and the narrowness of the roads now that they have been flooded."

He studied them a moment. She was correct. And it was an excellent observation. "Thank you for that."

He helped her down and turned to ask her to assess the needs of the families with him, but she had already headed away toward the first group on the lawn.

Nodding, he went the opposite direction in search of the vicar, knowing instinctually that she had things well in hand.

The vicar agreed with him and the need to move many of them to Pemberley. "I will keep as many as I can here at the vicarage. It will be closer for them to their homes. But the others need a place to stay. We could also use the schoolroom in town and the main hall."

"Yes, but I think they will do well in our great hall. We shall petition others to help our cook, and it shall be well." He gripped the good vicar's shoulder. "Thank you. You are an excellent shepherd for our flock here. And I know they are always in good hands."

"I am but a servant of the one good shepherd, and we are all doing our best." A maid approached, and he answered a question about linens then turned back to Arthur. "Shall we begin with the carts?"

"We should. We have the one. And it has supplies for you."

"Bless you. Your father is proud every day smiling down on you from heaven. I know he is."

"Thank you. I often wonder what he would do." He stepped nearer and lowered his voice. "You know Fitz has returned and is working to free more who are trapped. I see a change in him. I think he's ready."

"I can only hope. He will be a huge blessing when he's ready. I saw it in him as a lad. Such a good heart and a brilliant leader. He has an edge you don't have. Your softness serves you well, but his sharpness will also have a purpose."

Arthur didn't overanalyze the dear man's

assessment. He'd known him since he and Fitz were young lads, and he'd been telling them what to do for just as many years. He was good to the core, and Arthur trusted him.

They unloaded the wagon and sent the first family back to the house before he saw Miss Elizabeth again. And when he did, his heart warmed all over again. She had planted herself on the earth with a group of children all around her playing some game with rocks and sticks. He could only guess its purpose, but the children were enthralled. What was more intriguing to Darcy was the organization. The earlier chaos of arriving families was replaced by organized groups, everyone managing their belongings, looking ready to travel.

He shook his head in wonder. She was magnificent.

But Fitz had chosen her. His brother didn't love her. He didn't even know her. But he was a smart Darcy and had chosen her. He'd promised his brother a chance to win her over. He said they would talk this evening even if it was ridiculously late at night; he and Fitz would talk about what had transpired between him and Miss Elizabeth.

She obviously preferred Arthur. Didn't she? But she had agreed to come to dinner. She had been sitting at his side. They had a familiarity, a comfort that he wasn't certain he had ever attained with her.

What they had now was anything but comfortable. More like a rolling anthem about ready to crescendo in a great burst of noise over and over again. It was glorious. And anticipatory and beautiful.

But wasn't she just what his glorious childhood estate needed? Wasn't she the perfect woman to be Pemberley's mistress? Would she not mold Fitz into the man he could become?

His old friend, Duty, commenced a battle in his mind over what he needed and what the estate—what Fitz—needed. He was certain with Miss Elizabeth as Fitz's wife, Pemberley would thrive, blossom and grow. It would be protected for a multitude of generations to come.

But he, too, had an estate, a legacy to build, and a heart. He had a heart. And it just might break in two were he to give up Miss Elizabeth to the estate. He didn't know if he could ever do such a thing.

She would have to choose. It would certainly

rest in her heart to decide. It wasn't as if he was going to tell her who to love, was he? But he could express her options in a way that she saw the full and accurate picture. The wealth and opportunity from Pemberley far outweighed his own. They would be comfortable and it would grow, but it wasn't much compared to Pemberley.

What would his father say?

He had no idea. Would his father wish the heir to have the first pick of women?

Miss Elizabeth came to him then, cheeks flushed, eyes glowing, and as he reached for her hand in welcome, he knew right then he didn't care. He didn't care one whit what his father would have done or if she'd be better for Pemberley. He would do everything he could to win her no matter what it took.

"And how are things?" Her voice was bright and happy.

"We have begun the process of carting everyone back."

"So we are not as needed here?"

"I guess not, though there is always more to be done."

"I thought we might walk the roads a bit to

make sure there aren't some who haven't made it?"

He hesitated but a moment, thinking of the danger, discomfort, and growing chill, and then nodded. "Of course. I'll ask for two lanterns."

They could be walking for a long time in the dark, and the two of them couldn't do much to help anyone they found. But they would be able to go back for help. And perhaps they could bring some others.

Miss Elizabeth beckoned to someone and in a moment, three larger boys stood at his side. "These three would like to help anyone we find get back to here. I think with some extra muscle, we should be fine."

He could only nod, once again amazed at her ingenuity and planning. "I agree. Thank you to you three. Tell me your names."

They told him in turn. Brothers. Elijah, Malachi, and Isaiah. "Those are excellent, strong names."

"Our mama found them in the Bible, listening to our good vicar on Sundays." Elijah grinned. "She's real proud of that."

"As she should be." Miss Elizabeth reached for the lantern that someone had brought from the house. Darcy hefted the other. "Now let us be off. I heard of a particular street that might not have been cleared of everyone."

Everyone followed Miss Elizabeth who stepped away with determined strong steps out into the darkness. The light lit her face, and once again Darcy was enchanted. She was a beacon. The warm glow brought out the beauty in her features. He could have stared all evening.

They kept their voices down and listened as they walked. Every now and then Miss Elizabeth called out, "Hello! Is anybody there?"

House after house appeared empty. Miss Elizabeth walked slower and slower. With any luck, everyone had been cleared out and all were safe. She rubbed her arms under her coat.

"Are you taking a chill, Miss Elizabeth? I cannot forgive myself if you become ill. Perhaps we should return? We can ask the servants to do one more pass-through this evening?"

But then they heard scratching.

"Hello?" Miss Elizabeth hurried toward the sound. But after a few steps, she screamed and disappeared.

He ran forward, tripping on root branches and sliding on newer mud, bringing him to the edge of a hole of some sort. One of the boys behind him reached out to grab him by the collar.

He placed a hand on his shoulder. "Thank you." Then he yelled, "Miss Elizabeth!"

She moaned down below.

He lowered his lantern, trying to assess what he was seeing.

The other three approached carefully. "She's down there. I see her." Elijah pointed.

"Mama always said he could see in the dark." Malachi nudged him.

"Elizabeth." He pleaded with her in his mind to be well.

She didn't respond.

"I have to get down there." He turned to the boys. "Help lower me. Then you can run for help. But someone needs to be with her." He turned to lower his legs backward, reaching for their hands.

"Forgive me, Mr. Darcy, but you don't know where you're landing."

"Just make sure I don't land on her." He gritted his teeth as roots scratched at him through his shirt. He lowered himself as far as he could go, then grasping their hands, he was lowered a bit more before he said, "Let me drop. Then go for help."

They did, and the ground came sooner than he was expecting. "Oof."

"You alright, Mr. Darcy?"

"I am. Can you toss me the lantern?"

They did, and he caught the glowing object out of the darkness. It was an interesting experience to see only light coming toward you when all else was dark. He held it up. They were in a hole, with wet, slippery mud at his feet. "Elizabeth." He stepped carefully to the other side of the space.

She did not respond, and his heart nearly stopped. "Elizabeth. Can you hear me?"

He lifted her body in his arms just to hold her close. Her heart beat. She felt warm, though wet. "Let's get you dry. I'll hold you, darling. You are going to be well." He prayed his words would somehow come true simply by being spoken. He moved her to the least wet part of their hole and leaned her up against the wall of dirt. Then he shined the light on her, looking for cuts or bleeding or anything broken. She seemed to be free of anything obviously wrong. He cleared the hair from her face and placed the palm of his hand on her cheek. "Elizabeth, can you hear me?" He gave her shoulders a gentle shake. "Elizabeth, wake up. Come back. We have more work to do, don't you know?" His voice caught. The longer she remained unresponsive, the more his heart pounded. "Please." His throat tightened. He wiped some moisture from his eyes.

Then he ran hands down her arms, trying to keep her warm. He lifted her again and sat with her on his lap. "There. At least you'll be warm."

He cradled her close to his chest and rested his chin on the top of her head. It wouldn't be long. Then they could get her to safety and get her warm and the doctor would come and she would be fine. He hoped.

But time passed. More time than he thought should have.

Then drips of water started falling onto him. He held out a hand. "Rain?" He leaned his head back against the dirt wall. "No." He swallowed.

Elizabeth shifted against him. "Did you just say no?"

His mouth twitched. "Are you well? Elizabeth, are you awake?"

She nodded. "Barely." She shifted. "Am I... Am I sitting on your lap?" She lifted her head off

265

his chest and then groaned and lay it back against him. "I'm sorry. I can't move. Not yet."

"Stay still as long as you need. If I wasn't so frantically worried about you waking up, I would have enjoyed this situation above any other in my life."

She chuckled against him and then groaned again.

"What hurts?"

"My head. My...my side."

That didn't sound good. But at least she was speaking. "You fell. I think the ground just opened up?"

"It did. It felt like the ground just moved beneath me." She went still.

"Elizabeth?"

She didn't respond. "Elizabeth. Stay with me. Help is coming. Elizabeth. Keep talking."

She took a deep breath. "All right." She rubbed her nose. "I think there's someone else."

He lifted the lantern, looking around their space as best he could. "I don't see...wait. There is something."

"I heard scratching. I think I landed on him."

Darcy did not want to move, but he held up his lantern to try and get a better look.

"Looks like perhaps there is something over there. When help comes, we will take a look."

The raindrops became larger and more frequent. Somewhere in the pit the sound of actual falling water became a stream, pouring in.

"That doesn't bode well." He squinted up into the darkness. Their heads and upper bodies were somewhat shielded by a clump of dirt above them. But he was not unaware of the precarious situation. The pit could fill. A clump of dirt fell from the ledge above, landing on their feet. The whole thing could cave in on them, covering them.

"I knew you would come." Her soft voice warmed him to his toes. "I fell, but I knew it would be all right. You would come. You would find a way. You're like that."

He hugged her tighter against him. "I would do anything to keep you safe."

She snuggled in closer. "I know."

Her soft words, her confidence in him, the tenderness between them was the sweetest thing he'd ever experienced. It was as if a circle of love enveloped them, holding them close and warm even with the wet and cold all around them.

In that moment, he didn't think he could ever lose her. Here was the woman of his life, the mother of his children, the mistress of his estate, his partner and love. He swallowed. If he didn't love her yet, he knew it would be very easy to do so. He'd never met anyone of her caliber. The sincerity alone was enough to make him want to pursue her. She'd openly disliked and disapproved of him. His fingers cradled around her arms, gently holding her as best as he could. He hoped she was truly well. He would do all in his power to help her be so.

CHAPTER 24
ELIZABETH

Elizabeth knew that she hurt. She knew that breathing was challenging if she breathed too deeply. She knew that if she lifted her head again, the world would swim around her and might go dark. She knew that her head didn't feel precisely right. But she had never been more content than she felt in Mr. Darcy's arms. Everything was going to be just fine. How could it be otherwise when he was there?

But her mind kept swimming around thoughts and everything was as muddy as her cave. Was she in a cave? She didn't completely understand exactly where she was or how they were going to leave. But that was part of her confusion. Nothing worked in order. Didn't thoughts follow one another? Weren't they supposed to be in careful order?

Mr. Darcy's heartbeat pounded against her arm that rested on his chest. Its steady, fast, strong beating kept her brain in some sort of rhythm. Without its steadiness, she worried thoughts would spin round and round and out of control. But the constant sensation steadied her breathing, slowed her thoughts, and eventually led her own heart to beat in tune with his. She closed her eyes.

"Don't fall asleep." He shifted his chin on her head.

"I'm so tired. And you're so nice." She smiled. "You are better than my pillow. Maybe I shall use you from now on." She laughed to herself and then groaned. "Ow."

"Keep talking. I don't care what you say, in fact I'd quite enjoy if you keep flirting with me."

"I'm not... Oh my goodness. Mr. Darcy. I'm so sorry. I am not asking... I don't mean to presume. Oh please." She felt her face heat. Had she just invited Mr. Darcy to be her pillow, in her bed?

She wished to sleep now, for a long time. "I should stop talking. I really should."

"I'm enjoying this. Come now. What else could I be used for? A pillow is good. But I'm lumpy."

She began to protest.

"No, I am. Nothing like the soft down of most pillows. At least I hope not." He laughed. "What else could I do? I could be a door stopper for you."

"What?"

"Yes, when the door closes too soon and you're not through? No footman around and there it is, closing before its time. Someone has to take care of that."

She smiled against his chest. "A door stopper would be nice."

"What about a handkerchief?"

Her laugh burst out of her in surprise. "No. What a terrible thing for you. They are used for all manner of things."

"Yes, I see your point. I'd like to be your spare."

"My spare?"

"Yes, I always carry a spare. And that one

would just get to ride along with you wherever you went; close. You could take me out now and again. Sniff me if other odors were unpleasant, dab your face and forehead and...lips." He chuckled when she gasped. "And then you could place me back close to your heart. I'd like that."

"You are much more amusing than I ever imagined."

"I am speaking much more freely than I've ever spoken with anyone. Come now. What else could I be?"

She thought for a moment. "You could be my book reader."

He held her close. "Now that's a job I would gladly take. But it has to be near a fire, with your feet in my lap, a blanket draped over us both, a tray of delights from Cook, and snow. Outside. A gentle, quiet snow falling."

Her soft sigh made him warm all over again. "That sounds nice. Yes, that is your most important job."

"Oh, there could be better ones even than that."

She couldn't imagine a single other one.

"Certainly. I could be the man who says good morning."

She gasped. "Arthur."

The use of his name on her lips surprised her, but she could think of no other way to express her intimate surprise. "You shouldn't speak so."

"We're in a cave by ourselves. Now is the moment we may speak so."

She could see the logic in that. But then again, something about that felt dangerous. It wasn't clear. But something should be worrying her. She knew it, but couldn't feel it, not with Mr. Darcy saying such things.

"What would you say in the morning?"

"You mean, besides good morning?"

She laughed. "Yes, or is that all you would say?"

"Oh no. That is not all. But it might not be the same thing every day. Some mornings it could be something as simple as good morning, sunshine."

She nodded against his chest, too happy for words at the delightful turn of such a fantasy. For the reality of his thoughts was too good for words.

"But other mornings I might say something like, "You. Are. Beautiful.""

"Mm."

"Yes, and then other mornings I might say other things."

"You are done revealing your secrets?"

"Some are to be a surprise, and some might just have to be spontaneous, in the moment kinds of things."

"I appreciate that."

"Are you a spontaneous type of person, Miss Elizabeth?"

"Call me Lizzie."

He hesitated a moment and then repeated, "Lizzie."

A delicious thrill rushed through her. What a beautiful sound to hear his voice speak her most intimate name. She breathed in and out two full times, savoring it. "I am spontaneous."

He smiled. She could feel the movement of his jaw.

"But other times I'm a planner."

"I can see that."

"Yes, well, if a person thinks a thing through for but a moment, everything might flow all the better for it."

"I completely agree. And yet some things are

moments for immediate action, and so one must not be held up by the planning."

"Certainly not. But it doesn't take very long to plan. I think you can be both."

"I agree with you. I think everyone should be a little bit of both."

"I'm afraid I'm a lot spontaneous and only a small portion planner."

"So, if we were walking along, and it was a hot day, would you jump into the pond?"

She considered him a moment. Dare she admit?

"I would, and I have."

"You have? Which pond is this?"

"There is one not too far from my house." She considered her next words but then giggled. "And I had to undress a bit to do it."

He made a mock gasping sound. "Miss Elizabeth Bennet, you did not."

"I did, and I'm proud of it." She pressed her lips together. "Although I never imagined telling anyone else, and I'm not sure how I feel about that part."

"I shall only think the best things about you no matter what you tell me. I give my word." He laughed and then whispered, "I think even better of you knowing you did such a thing."

"I like that."

"Why are you pleased?"

"I think I would most enjoy a relationship with someone who could know me fully, completely, and love me." She almost bit the words back in, but they were said and there was nothing further to be done, so she kept talking. "And, of course, know that I'm not perfect. I do silly things, annoying things, unwise things I'm certain, though I can't think of anything particular at the moment."

He reached for her hand and laced their fingers together. "I am certain you are not often unwise."

He was quiet a moment and then he said, "I wish I was a better brother."

"I am certain you are almost always the best brother in the world."

"Fitz." He sighed. "Georgiana." He breathed deeply, trying to express what he hadn't even really realized about himself until that moment. "If I did less for them, they would be better."

She nodded. "They are quite remarkable, you know."

"I do. I think I'm realizing that more about Fitz. I was quite surprised at his choice to stay in at dinner. But then I realized he was not being negligent. It wasn't himself he was putting first." He cleared his throat. "It was you."

She nodded against him.

"Is there... Do you...?" He sighed.

"No." She squeezed his hand. "There is no understanding between us. There is only simply a dinner invitation."

He leaned his head back in relief. "All the same, he is quite impressed."

"He does not know me at all."

"Oh, but I'm certain he does. You are quite impressive upon first meeting."

She shook her head. "Do you want to know what I overheard him say when he first saw me?"

He groaned. "I'm not certain I do."

"Perhaps I'll have him tell you when we are all together next." She lifted their hands. "Fitz is not even remotely enamored with me."

Arthur held her closer again, running his thumb over the back of her glove. "I am dreading the time when you will be lifted from my arms, but at the same time, I'm becoming concerned.

They should be back by now. We need to get you warm and call the doctor. With any luck, he is already at the house."

"I hope all is well up there."

A cold, wet something nudged her arm. She yelped. "What is that?" She twisted, ignoring the sharp pains that shot through her. A soft head with a cold, wet nose rested in her lap. "Well, hello there."

"Is this a dog?"

"I'm almost certain."

He held up the lamp. "Yes. A very mangy-looking dog."

"Oh, don't insult him so. We are partners in this pit. He's perfectly adorable."

"Yes, adorable." He pet the pup's head. "So it was for you we ended up here?"

"I think so."

The dog whimpered.

"Oh, don't you worry. We're with Mr. Darcy. Everything is going to be just fine."

Distant voices brought a feeling of relief and dread all at once. "I think they are coming."

"Yes."

For a moment, neither said anything. But

then Arthur pressed his mouth to the top of her head. "Will you be all right if I stand?"

"I think so."

He used his shoulder to brace against the muddy wall and rose with her in his arms. Then he placed her back on the ground. The dog snuggled right up next to her.

Arthur called out, "We're here! Over here. Come quick!"

The voices got closer, and soon a light bobbed above them.

"Arthur."

"Fitz." The relief in Arthur's voice made Elizabeth smile. He loved his brother, and he relied on him.

A rope dropped down to them. Arthur helped her stand. "Let's get you out of here first."

She nodded and clung to him, the world spinning crazily about her. "I'm so dizzy."

"We will get you taken care of." He tied the rope about her waist. "Hang on to this."

She gripped the rough fibers through her gloves.

"She's ready."

Soon she was lifted in the air, steadily,

slowly and then into the arms of Fitz. "Are you well?"

"I think so?"

Other hands guided her to a cart and wrapped her in blankets. Someone handed her a warm bowl. "Drink this."

The warm fluid went down in a beautiful thickness that sent warm tendrils throughout her body. She smiled. "Thank you." The blanket, the warmth, the safe feeling brought such a drowsy feeling, she closed her eyes.

"Don't let her fall asleep," a familiar voice called out.

She whipped her eyes open.

And then a dog jumped up beside her. "Oh, hello. Didn't I tell you Mr. Darcy would get you out?"

And then a maid climbed up beside her with a young child in her arms. "And this little fellow was down there too."

"What!" She couldn't believe it.

"The dog showed Mr. Darcy."

"Is he... Will he be all right?"

"He's breathing. He is warming up. The doctor is at the house waiting."

She nodded. What a strange thing to

happen. What a beautiful, magnificent, horrible, wonderful thing to happen to a person. She smiled to herself and drank more of the soup. She didn't have any energy to think about what it all meant. She focused on staying awake and watching the child for any signs of life. Thanks to Arthur, everyone was going to be well. They had to be.

CHAPTER 25
ARTHUR

Arthur paced in frustration outside Elizabeth's room.

The doctor had come and gone, and all he'd heard was that she was fine. She would be fine. She just needed rest. He would have to wait before she was able to receive visitors. They were about to give her some laudanum for some much-needed sleep.

All her sisters were in there right now, saying goodnight. His sister was in there. The maids were in there. His housekeeper too, even the dog had been given entrance. All except for Darcy were with Elizabeth.

He paced again.

Fitz came around the corner. "Banned from the room?"

"Abominably."

"Brother. Since when are you commanded about by a bunch of servants?"

"Since...now." He stood taller. "You are most correct, Fitz. I think it is high time I exerted my position in this house."

"Absolutely."

They stood together a moment, Fitz watching Arthur with narrowed eyes. "You love her?"

"I do."

"I don't. I could have, mind you. I could have loved that woman."

"I hope you do."

When Fitz widened his eyes, Arthur laughed. "As a sister. If she will have me, I plan to never be parted from her again from this day on."

He nodded. "I approve. I will heartily welcome her to Pemberley."

After a moment more, Arthur gripped his shoulder. "I think we will be making our way to Rosewood House."

Fitz eyed him a moment and then nodded. "I won't do everything the same way you do it."

"I expect not."

"You going to be able to let it go?"

"It's time. I'm most anxious to. Lizzie helps. We have our own estate to create, to grow, to work on side by side."

"Can you also relax and throw a ball or two?"

"Ball! That's for you at Pemberley. If we ever clear out the neighborhood from our great room, you can hold our engagement ball."

"I suppose I shall alert the staff."

"Wait. I haven't proposed."

"You don't think she'll say no, do you?"

"I think we are much aligned in our thinking. I hope nothing has changed that in the few hours we have been parted. Much of what she admitted was under the influence of a head injury while stuck at the bottom of a pit."

Fitz laughed. "Well, that's one way." He raised an eyebrow. "Everyone would keep it quiet. You do this of your own will, I gather?"

"I do. She is the one of my choice, my heart."

He nodded. "Then I wish you the happiest of times. Now, come. They are crowding her. It is high time you had your moment." He stepped to the door, opening it wide. "Time to leave Miss Elizabeth be." He lifted a hand.

They stood in surprise but nodded. "You are so right, Mr. Darcy." Miss Mary winked at him, eyeing Arthur.

They filed out of the room. The housekeeper glared. But Fitz shooed Arthur in and left the door open a crack.

He stepped closer to the bed. She was covered to her neck in blankets. The room felt cozy and warm. She was rosy and washed. And watching him approach.

"Are you well?" He moved to stand beside her, suddenly insecure. The security of the dark, the feeling of her in his arms were not emboldening as they had been before.

She scooted over and made room for him so he sat beside her at the edge of the bed. "Miss Elizabeth..."

Her eyes twinkled a moment and then she whispered, "Lizzie."

The smile spread across the whole bottom part of his face. He felt it tight and happy. "Lizzie."

She nodded. "I'm about to feel very drowsy, they tell me, so this should be quick. Because I also might start saying and admitting things again that are completely unfair for you to know."

"But they might be things that I love most about you."

Her eyes shone in response. She watched him. "Love?"

"I do, Lizzie. I love you. There is much more to say and many more dreams of mine to express. But for now, sleep well in the knowledge that I love you. I think I always will."

"I love you, too." She closed her eyes. "Like the clouds and the junipers and the flowers on the way..." She stopped talking.

He smiled and ran a hand along her forehead. "Sleep well, my Lizzie."

As soon as he exited, their maid entered. "Thank you for caring for her. Treat her as you would a Darcy."

She nodded and curtseyed. Then she paused. "She says your name in her sleep." Her smile slipped out.

He laughed.

But Fitz shook his head at the maid. "That will be forgiven once, but that's her business. We don't share the private things with others, do we?"

She dipped her head. "No, we don't. Forgive me. I thought Mr. Darcy would be happy to hear it. And it's a night that's needing much cheer."

Arthur smiled. "Mr. Darcy is correct, but thank you."

She bobbed another curtsey and then hurried in.

"Well-spoken Fitz. You really will be the best heir of Pemberley."

"You good with that?"

"I am at last satisfied with being the spare."

Fitz pulled him close. "Thank you. I am at last ready to be the heir."

"I'm missing our parents." He glanced back over his shoulder at Lizzie's door.

"They would have loved her."

"I think you're right. Mother would have enjoyed her strength and fiery personality."

"Fiery?"

Arthur laughed at his brother's confused expression. "You really don't know her at all, do you?"

He shrugged.

"Well, yes. She has a strong personality and a soft one and a perfectly lovely one." With an arm across Fitz's shoulders, they walked down the hall toward the study.

"And now I have to see about whether or not I can get a special license."

"And perhaps you should write her parents?"

"Oh, yes. You've met them. What am I to think?"

Fitz hesitated but a moment and then smiled. "You will love them."

CHAPTER 26

ELIZABETH

A week in bed and she was more restless than she had ever been. A maid helped dress her for her first outing, and it was going to be a good long one. She swished her skirts. "This is a lovely color, don't you think?"

"It matches your eyes. Miss Georgiana's too, when she wears it."

"I think it would make her look more beautiful than ever."

"And it does the same for you, miss." The maid who had been helping her was becoming a trusted advisor in everything that had to do with the Darcy household. And she appreciated every word.

"Now, you know I'm not supposed to be saying anything. Mr. Darcy has strict rules about keeping everyone's privacy..." She looked around dramatically as if someone in the room might be hearing her. "But he did ask me to treat you extra special, like you were already a Darcy."

Lizzie grinned. "I'm absolutely certain you were not supposed to tell me that."

"Oh, they know I can't keep secrets." She winked. "Which means, you were supposed to hear it!"

"Wait. Are you telling everyone my secrets?"

"Not at all, miss. I was told really and truly to keep yours. He was kind of forceful about it. I was quite surprised."

"Who?"

"Mr. Darcy, the heir, miss. He reminded me my place and told me your privacy was private or I wouldn't be the one hired to help you." She curtseyed. "If you approve, of course." She colored. "And you agree to marry him." She placed a hand on her lips. "We all love you, miss. We hope you say yes. We're just so sad to see Mr. Darcy go. But I hear his estate is just lovely. And it will be all your own."

Lizzie couldn't believe the audacity of this

maid. She surely could not keep a secret. "Thank you. I love you all dearly. And the tenants. I think we all have become close living here together like this."

"And the Darcys are the best people that ever were, miss. All of us feel blessed to be here." She finished the last of Lizzie's hair, curled around her face and piled on her head.

Lizzie turned this way and that, admiring. "You work wonders, my dear. Thank you."

She stood, not feeling a bit of the dizziness that had plagued her whenever she stood all week. "I think I'm getting much better."

"Your color has certainly returned. You're the most beautiful I've ever seen you." She smiled with such warmth, Lizzie had to love her, loose tongue and all.

"Could you let them all know I'm ready?"

"I expect he shall meet you at the front door?"

Lizzie shook her head. "Just let them know, please." She was inordinately pleased to know something her maid did not know. With a huge grin, she slipped out the door and down the hall.

The barn was close. As soon as she stepped

in the door, Mangy jumped up on her, licking her furiously.

His owner, the lad from the pit, Heath, called to her. "Oh, stop that. She's got a pretty dress on today, you mutt, can't you see?"

"He's just fine. We love this mangy mutt, don't we?"

"Yeah, he's alright." Heath stood in front of Lizzie. "Are you going out in the carriage, then?"

"We are. For a picnic and a journey to see the other house. I'm quite excited to see it."

"It fits you."

"Have you seen it?"

"I have. I like it better than Pemberley, though we aren't supposed to have favorites."

"I think we can have favorites, why not?"

He shrugged.

The stablemaster called out, "Heath!"

He bowed and scrambled back to the horses.

She turned in a circle, breathing in the delicious smells of the barn. Arthur was going to meet her there. She wanted to bring the dog with them.

Lizzie felt him before she saw him, the hair on her arms flirting delightfully with the breeze and standing up in expectation. "My maid didn't know we were meeting here." She turned.

"Oh?" His eyes lit in appreciation as he saw her. "Did we manage to keep something from her?"

"We did."

He smiled and reached for her hand. "You are so beautiful. This dress suits you."

"Georgiana is so kind to share."

"I think she'd give you half her clothes. It's part of the fun of having a sis—another woman in the house." His face colored in an adorable pink, and she let his almost slip go without comment. But a thrill rushed through her.

"I can't express how happy I am to be out of the house. I cannot wait for this outing, to feel the beautiful breeze, to see the countryside, and to experience your home." She swallowed back a bit of emotion. "I can't think of a time I've been more excited."

He pulled her close and then into an embrace. "I want nothing more than to share it all with you. Shall we?"

She nodded against him. "Can we keep the window shades open?"

He grinned. "Of course."

"And let Mangy ride with us?"

"I had them bathe him just for this moment."

"Perfect." She linked their fingers, and as their hands swayed between them, they made their way out the barn doors to the carriage.

As the doors opened, more than just the carriage awaited. Her parents; all her sisters; the Lucases—even Charlotte and Mr. Collins; and a sour-faced woman who must be Lady Catherine greeted her. The carriage was covered in spring flowers of all kinds making their first appearance—many from her beautiful Longbourne, some from Pemberley, and some from other exotic places. It smelled of a beautiful garden.

She clasped her hands together. "This is the most beautiful thing I have ever seen." She hurried to hug her mother and father who kissed her head.

"I'm so grateful you are well." The tears in his eyes warmed her heart.

"Thank you, Papa."

Jane ran to her then, with Mr. Bingley in tow. "We have something to announce later."

"Then today will be the happiest I can possibly imagine."

Jane's eyes filled with tears. "For me as well." She kissed Lizzie's cheek.

Mary hugged her tight. And close behind Mary stood Mr. Miller, the vicar from the house party. "Now that's a man I am very pleased to see." And behind him, Lord Shackley.

Lizzie laughed. "Oh, I'm so pleased to see you!"

He nodded. "As am I to see you."

Lydia and Kitty both squeezed her tight, though Lydia did not look convinced.

"I promise, with the right person this is lovely, indeed."

A flicker of hope lit her face, and she nodded.

And then the door opened, and Arthur helped her up.

As they drove away, everyone she most loved waving and smiling, she turned to Arthur, unable to stop her tears. "What a lovely surprise. Will we dine with them tonight?"

"Yes, I think they are staying for a bit." His eyes held promises. She let those soak deep inside her. Unspoken, she heard them, cradled them, allowed them to fill in all the cracks of loneliness she'd always known and settle inside.

Two footmen and a coachman traveled with

them. A maid sat up top. The windows were wide open, and the breeze smelled of the flowers that covered the carriage.

"This is quite a flower feat. I love it so much."

"I'm so glad. I know how much you love flowers."

"I really do. How far are we going?"

"It will take a couple of hours. And in that time..." He pulled out some books. "I have come to fulfill my promise as your book reader."

She laughed.

"No fire or blanket today."

"But that can come."

"Yes, it most certainly can." His gaze filled her with warmth. She daringly kicked off her slippers and rested her feet in Arthur's lap. "What are you reading today?"

After many pages of *Sense and Sensibility*, which left the both of them quite in angst and frustration about the fate of dear Elenor, they put the book aside. "We are arriving near the estate."

She rushed to the side of the carriage near him and peered out the window. Everything about them was green. Everywhere they looked, fields and fields of rolling green hills and low stone walls poured over the world like a blanket.

"It's amazing. I wish to walk over the whole of it."

"I'll join you. Might we also ride?"

She laughed. "Of course."

They peered together out the carriage window, Arthur pointing to things, or Lizzie pointing to things, and both completely contented with everything around them.

They turned down a drive and continued on in between a row of trees with a high stone wall running down one side.

She breathed in great contentment. "Everything here is so peaceful."

"The fountains, rose gardens, and greenhouse are even more so. I do hope you like it, that you approve." His eyes filled with so much hope, yet with a touch of insecurity—so much so that she wished to kiss it away.

Completely embarrassed by her thoughts, she tried to hide the blush by looking out the window again, but Arthur turned her head to face him again. "With me, there is never anything to fear, no need to be embarrassed, and an openness to say and act freely, please." He pleaded with his expression, and Lizzie didn't quite know what to do.

She laughed. "Oh, Mr. Darcy. Some things are best shared after an anticipating wait."

He moved closer to her than he ever had, so close that she could feel his breath on her skin. "I could not agree more. I shall have to wait and it shall be ever sweeter because of it."

Her whole head pounded with the beating of her heart. She swallowed and then tried to wet her very dry mouth. "Well then, Mr. Darcy, shall we see your grand estate, then?"

He waved the footman over who opened the carriage door then swung down quickly to turn and offer his hand to Lizzie. "Yes, we shall. But it's not like Pemberley. Please know that it will grow..."

"Oh, my Darcy. It is far better."

He opened his mouth to protest.

But she held up a finger. "Because you have created it, and for that, I shall treasure it as a part of you always."

He stood so still she wondered if he'd forgotten to breathe and then wiped his eyes with the back of his hands. "Let's be off then, please may I escort you?"

"Yes, my good Mr. Darcy."

"Why all this Mr. Darcy all of a sudden?"

She shrugged. "I like it. And now that I know the preferred Mr. Darcy, I love it even more."

"At least call me Arthur sometimes."

She just grinned.

He led her straight up the stairs where it looked like his entire staff waited outside to meet them. Their livery was a deep royal blue with white trim. Sun gleamed off of the buttons. A woman and man stepped forward, presumably the housekeeper and butler.

"Mrs. Wilkins. Hobson. I'd like you to meet a woman who is very special to me and to my family. Miss Elizabeth Bennet."

The curtsey and bow from the two very proper and stately servants were also kind in their own way. The two main household staff seemed to be the good, solid sort of no-nonsense workers that Elizabeth knew she could respect and appreciate if given the chance.

Everything was so obviously important to Arthur. She knew he cared. She saw where this was heading. And she was overly excited. This life, this man, this estate; she would never have guessed that one day she'd be so fortunate. And to marry for love. What a gift, indeed. Her smile filled her face and she didn't even attempt to dim it.

"And what are you smiling about?" Arthur laced their fingers together.

"I'm just happy."

"So this pleases you?"

"Oh, yes. I don't think I've ever seen a situation quite so pleasing."

He laughed. "I hope very much that you like it."

They walked through the house together, touring every room, Arthur asking Lizzie's thoughts on colors and furniture. The adjoining master suites filled one wing of the upstairs with sitting rooms and large closets and servants' quarters and an oversized bath. They moved to the grounds and the many gardens around the home, and the barn. Inside a horse knickered, and Arthur introduced her to a horse that would be just right for her. The animal nuzzled her palm. They moved out around the side of the house to a gate to a walled-in space.

He turned the key and pushed open a door to a small inner courtyard with a fountain. The walls were lined with beds of flowers. A tree rose up in the corner and from one of its branches, a swing moved gently in the breeze. The grass was soft. The earth smelled lovely, and even in the chill of the evening air they'd been having, everything seemed to be thriving. She smiled and breathed it in. "Now this place, I could spend every day of the rest of my life." She spun in a slow circle, wanting to take everything in, one bud at a time.

"It would be for your own particular use, though I might visit you from time to time?" He grinned and pointed to a door leading into the house. "That is your study, with a starter library of books."

She blinked back tears at this point. "Mr. Darcy. It is all too much. I don't need... That is, we haven't specifically discussed this, but I don't need any of this to make me happy. I would spend the rest of my days quite satisfied with just you." A tear ran down her cheek which he quickly wiped away.

"What is this? Tears, my dear?"

She nodded. "You are too good."

He shook his head. "It is my opinion that nothing could be too good for you. Now, please, if you can indulge me, I wanted to be right here when I asked this question." He dropped down to one knee in the soft earth in front of her. The fountain trickled water behind her. The sun shone in dappled rays through the trees. The flowers scented the air. And Lizzie was overcome.

"Lizzie, would you please do me the honor of being my wife? I cannot promise the decades of history of a grand estate, but instead one of new beginnings and a strong and willing heart at your side."

Happiness filled her as well as what felt like every other emotion. She struggled to even swallow. Wiping at the tears on her face, she nodded. "Yes. I will do everything I can to fill your life with sunshine." She rested a hand at the side of his face. "You are so deserving of it." She kneeled down at his front, their faces level, his tender eyes staring into her own. "I love you, Arthur."

His smile filled his face and he closed his eyes. "The sweetest words ever spoken to me." He took her face in his hands, gently running fingers down the sides of her cheeks and then through her hair. "I love you too, my Lizzie. Thank you for making me the happiest of men."

His eyes shown with the joy that coursed

between them. Then his gaze moved to her lips. He captured them within moments, wrapping his other arm around her back. When she leaned into him, returning all her affection as best she could, he kissed her over and over, pulling and nibbling and pressing until she was quite content to stay in his arms forever. He rested his forehead against hers, slightly out of breath and very clearly wanting to keep kissing her. "And now, the rest of that will have to wait."

She giggled out of pure embarrassment that he'd dare bring up anything of the kind in conversation.

But he just laughed and then he swung her up into his arms. "I would like to show you your personal study."

She wrapped her arms around his neck while he carried her through the door to her own library and received a very thorough tour of a small study, in between a very thorough round of kisses. He pulled her into his lap on a lovely oversized chair, both laughing at the enjoyment and freedom of it all.

"So is this what life with you will be like, my Darcy?"

He pulled her closer. "And more. So much

more. I promise to love you and laugh with you and probably cry with you until the day we die."

She rested her head on his shoulder, perfectly content with that picture of how her life would be. "How soon can we be married?"

She felt his chuckle all through her body as he rested his chin on top of her head. "As soon as you like."

EPILOGUE

Fitz felt manipulated into planning and hosting a huge engagement ball for his brother. Certainly they must have one, but he, Fitz, would just as soon be anywhere else.

He stood at attention next to his brother and Miss Elizabeth, and he had to grudgingly admit that she was much better for him than she would have been for himself. She was, in fact, somewhat demanding, and he would have tired of her own excellence which would have urged him to be better all the time. Were there not moments when one and all should rest?

"Brother, you are frowning." Miss Elizabeth placed a gentle hand on his arm.

"I must not be feeling overly pleased."

She laughed. "Come now. It cannot be as bad as all that. Your servants have handled all the details. And surely there is someone here who is handsome enough to tempt you?" Her eyebrow rose in a wicked challenge.

He groaned.

"What is this?" Arthur stepped closer. "What do you mean handsome enough?"

Miss Elizabeth smiled. "That's a story best heard from the lips of Fitz himself."

He sighed. "It is not the large upheaval she makes of it."

"Oh, but I think it is. I suspect it is the very thing that almost kept us apart."

She nodded. "Partly, yes."

Fitz rubbed the spot between his eyes. "I was tired. I did not feel like dancing, and Bingley was a pest. So I told him that your Lizzie was handsome but not enough to tempt me." He winced. "Brother, please do not pummel me at your own party."

Arthur grew still.

But Lizzie leaned closer and kissed his cheek. "I was mad enough for the both of us. Let us forget it ever happened."

"Fitz will suffer for that." Arthur stood taller. "Be aware, brother, there will be consequences."

"Of that I'm certain." He leaned closer to Lizzie. "Not sure why I deserved that."

"Just some sisterly teasing. It comes with the territory, I'd imagine." She looked past him. "Oh, look alive. Here is someone I would like for you to meet."

Miss Vincent had outdone herself. She stood tall and flowing and ethereal as she floated into the room and joined the line of greeters.

Fitz followed her gaze and then remained riveted on her. "Who is this?"

"That, my dear brother, is Miss Vincent and the only person I can countenance you marrying."

He tutted at that. "You, my sister, do not get a choice. But she is most definitely handsome enough." He visibly swallowed and straightened his coat.

When Miss Vincent was close enough, Lizzie embraced her. "Oh, it is good to see you."

"And you. So pleased that I could witness the beginning."

"I, as well. Now, might I introduce you to

Darcy's brother?" She placed a hand on Fitz's arm.

"Goodness me. You're a twin." She looked from one to the other. "And I met the other?"

Arthur stepped forward. "You did, indeed. It is so good to see you."

She received his bow and then turned to Fitz. "And you are someone I find myself interested in knowing."

He opened his mouth and then closed it again. Then he cleared his throat. Lizzie nudged him. "I, as well. Rather, I'd like to meet you, to know you." He looked away. "Would you save me a dance?"

She nodded with a wink to Lizzie. "I would like that."

"Thank you."

Many minutes after she moved down the line, Fitz watched her wherever she went in the room and when, at last, the music began and the line of greeters dwindled enough, he went immediately to her side.

Luckily, his ability to speak had returned by then.

Lizzie watched them together. "I do like Miss Vincent."

THE HEIR AND SPARE

"As do I. But you know we can't be choosing Fitz's wife."

"And why not?" She laughed. "No, I know. But I do believe they've made a good beginning of it, don't you?"

"I do." He pulled her close. "And now, might I dance with my fiancé?"

"You might." She placed her hands in his. "How soon is the wedding day?"

"Ten days."

She sighed. "What if we just showed up at the church and asked Mr. Miller to marry us forthwith?"

"And then host a ball on the wedding day but not tell everyone that we're already married?"

She laughed. "Something like that, yes." Her eyebrows raised in challenge. "I don't know if I want to wait ten days."

"Nor do I." He lifted her fingers to his lips. "But at least you are here at Pemberley. I couldn't abide you being at Longbourne."

"Nor I."

He spun her in a circle just the two of them before joining a line of people to begin their dance. "I love you, my Lizzie."

The End.

Do you like *Pride and Prejudice* retellings? I have another. You can find *Handsome Enough* HERE.

FOLLOW JEN

Some of Jen's other published books

The Duke's Second Chance
The Earl's Winning Wager
Her Lady's Whims and Whimsies
Suitors for the Proper Miss
Pining for Lord Lockhart
The Foibles and Follies of Miss Grace

The Nobleman's Daughter
Two lovers in disguise

Scarlet
The Pimpernel retold

A Lady's Maid
Can she love again?

His Lady in Hiding
Hiding out as his maid.

Spun of Gold
Rumpelstilskin Retold

Dating the Duke
Time Travel: Regency man in NYC

Charmed by His Lordship
The antics of a fake friendship

Tabitha's Folly
Four over-protective brothers

To read Damen's Secret
The Villain's Romance

Follow her Newsletter

www.ingramcontent.com/pod-product-compliance
Lightning Source LLC
Chambersburg PA
CBHW070916260626
47162CB00007B/2691